The Blackwing Puzzle

The phone rang and Joe hurried to pick it up. The caller was Jeff Allen, owner of the old Blackwing Mansion.

"Could you fellows come over right away?"

"Sure," Joe said. "Something wrong?"

"It's the ghost," Jeff said. "It's come back!"

The Hardys hurried outside and went whizzing off in their yellow sports car. The moon was bright and nearly full. As they reached Indian Road and approached the Allens' house, Frank gasped. "Look there, Joe! Just ahead!"

A black-winged creature could be seen, clearly silhouetted in the moonlight, as it soared above the treetops!

The Hardy Boys Mystery Stories

Available from MINSTREL Books

82

The HARDY BOYS®

THE BLACKWING PUZZLE

FRANKLIN W. DIXON

A MINSTREL® BOOK

PUBLISHED BY POCKET BOOKS

New York   London   Toronto   Sydney   Tokyo   Singapore

A Minstrel Book published by
POCKET BOOKS, a division of Simon & Schuster Inc.,
1230 Avenue of the Americas, New York, NY 10020

ISBN: 0-671-70472-9

First Minstrel Books printing September 1987

10 9 8 7 6 5 4 3 2

THE HARDY BOYS MYSTERY STORIES, A MINSTREL BOOK
and colophon are trademarks of Simon & Schuster Inc.

THE HARDY BOYS is a registered trademark
of Simon & Schuster Inc.

Printed in the U.S.A.

Contents

THE BLACKWING PUZZLE

1 Omen of Evil

"What sort of haunted house are we going to?" blond, seventeen-year-old Joe Hardy asked his brother as they drove through the streets of Bayport one morning.

"You've seen it," Frank replied. "It's the old Blackwing Mansion on Indian Road."

"Oh, yes—the one with the black-winged figure over the gateposts."

"Right. It used to belong to a slave-ship captain, or 'blackbirder' as they were called. In fact, I think that thing over the gateposts was actually the figurehead of his ship."

"Wow! The place must be pretty ancient!" said Joe.

3

Frank nodded as he turned their yellow sports sedan into Indian Road. "The house was built before the Civil War, which makes it well over a hundred years old . . . going on a century and a half, in fact. Of course, the young couple who own it now—the Allens—had it completely restored before they moved in."

"They're the ones who phoned us?" Joe asked.

"Yes—or at least the husband did, Jeff Allen."

"Any details on the haunting?"

"Not really," Frank replied. "All I know is that something spooky and very unpleasant's been happening at night, which has them pretty disturbed."

Joe shot his brother a half-humorous, half-quizzical glance. "What do they expect us to do—exorcise the house?"

Frank, who was eighteen, chuckled. "I doubt it. When Allen called, I told him bluntly that we don't believe in ghosts. I guess they don't, either. The point is, whatever's going on, they don't know what to make of it. It's a total mystery, so they're hoping we can solve it."

Though they were still in their teens, the Hardy boys had acquired a growing reputation as talented young sleuths. Their father, Fenton Hardy, a former ace detective of the New York

4

Police Department, had moved to the seaside town of Bayport and was now a famous private investigator. Frank and Joe seemed to be following in his footsteps and had already unraveled a number of baffling mysteries.

They rode along Indian Road, which lay in an older part of town, almost within sight of the bay and densely clustered with tall oaks and evergreens.

Frank slowed as they came to Blackwing Mansion and turned in to the graveled driveway, then braked to a halt so he and his brother could study the sinister figurehead that had given the house its name.

Though the huge carving had doubtlessly been inspired by the term "blackbird," it did not represent a raven or any other member of the crow family. Its weird head and torso and cruelly grasping talons made it appear to be a fearsome black demon. It had been mounted in such a way that its outspread wings formed a sinister arch over the two stone gateposts.

"Boy! How'd you like to have that thing swoop down on you in a dark alley?" said Joe with a slightly nervous laugh.

"No, thanks," Frank said wryly, starting up the car again. "Not even on a sunny street in the center of town!"

5

The house itself, which stood at the top of the drive backed against a hillside, was a beautifully restored Early Victorian mansion, with a square tower and tall, pointed eaves decorated with elaborate gingerbread scrollwork.

As the boys got out of their car and approached the house, the front door opened. A tall, good-looking young man in his early thirties, with curly brown hair, stepped out to greet them and shake hands. "Good of you fellows to come over on such short notice," he said.

"Well, it sounded like a mighty interesting case, Mr. Allen," Frank said after introducing their host to Joe.

"It's interesting, all right"—Jeff Allen smiled dryly—"but Mary and I won't mind a bit if we never see that Blackwing ghost again!"

He led the way into the spacious living room, where his wife, a slender, pretty young woman, had laid out coffee and cookies in anticipation of the boys' visit. When they were all seated and Mrs. Allen had served the refreshments, Frank began.

"What exactly is this Blackwing ghost you mentioned?"

"I just wish we knew!" she said with a shudder.

"You saw the figurehead over the gateposts?"

her husband added. "Well, we've seen that flying over the house at night—or something very much like it!"

The Hardy boys exchanged startled glances. "Are you serious?" Joe asked.

Jeff Allen shrugged. "Believe it or not, it's true, no matter how crazy it may sound. We've seen a weird creature not only flying but actually *hovering* over this house!"

"Are you sure it wasn't an unusually large crow, or maybe some kind of hawk?" Frank inquired.

Allen shook his head scornfully. "No way! You've seen the wingspread on that ship's figurehead over the gateposts—it must be at least twelve to fifteen feet wide. Well, this black apparition we keep seeing is *at least* that huge!"

"Excuse me if I seem to be doubting your word, Mr. Allen," Frank persisted. "But are you certain that you can judge size accurately when an object's high overhead . . . especially at night?"

"No offense taken, Frank—and by the way, please call me Jeff, not Mr. Allen. I started out as a surveyor before I got my degree in architecture, which is my present profession. You can take my word for it that my judgment of dimensions, even at a distance, is a good deal better than most people's."

7

"In any case, it's not only what we've seen but what we've *heard*," said Mary Allen. Her hand was trembling as she set down her coffee cup.

"What Mary means," Jeff added, "is that we've actually heard Captain Blackwing's voice—usually just before the ghost appeared."

"Heard him how?" said Joe.

"Right here in the house, as if he were walking around upstairs. He talks in a loud, rough voice, bellowing out commands to his crew from the quarterdeck. And sometimes his language isn't too nice!"

"And you're sure no one's hiding in the place?"

"Positive! There are no secret rooms or hidey-holes, either. I know because I studied the original blueprints when I was planning the restoration work."

Mr. Allen explained that the first time they heard the voice, they made a hasty search for intruders and looked out the windows to see if any prankster was lurking outside. "That was when we noticed Blackwing's shadow moving over the ground—as if some huge winged creature was hovering overhead. We looked upward, and there it was, silhouetted in the moonlight!"

There was a brief, startled silence. Both Frank

8

and Joe were baffled by the Allens' story. It was clear from Mrs. Allen's pale face and nervous manner that she was highly upset by the situation.

"You called that slaver Captain Blackwing," Joe said. "Was that his name?"

"No, his real name was Moray Thaw. He must have been a pretty nasty character. His neighbors despised him as an ex–slave trader who made his fortune out of human misery, and would have nothing to do with him. As the story goes, Captain Thaw returned their dislike and deliberately mounted that figurehead over the gateposts just to show his contempt for them."

The doorbell rang. Jeff Allen went to answer it and came back holding an envelope.

"Who was it, dear?" his wife asked.

"The mailman, with a special delivery letter."

"Something important?"

"Don't know. It's addressed to both of us." He opened and read the letter, then handed it to his wife with a frown. She gasped at its contents, and her face took on a strained, anxious expression. "Perhaps the Hardys should read it, too," Allen suggested.

Frank and Joe were astonished as they stared at the message. The sheet of stationery bore the

heading *MADAME XAVIA, Psychic Consultant*.
She wrote:

Dear Mr. and Mrs. Allen,
Although you may not know me, I beg
you to take seriously what I say. My gift of
seeing the unseen has shown me an *ominous black cloud of trouble* hanging over
your house. *I urge you to move out of it at
once!* Please call on me for whatever help or
advice I may be able to offer.

Yours sincerely,
Xavia

"Psychic consultant, huh?" Joe muttered
scornfully. "Sounds to me like a phony fortune-
teller trying to drum up business!"

"Perhaps so, but that reference to a black
cloud hanging over the house is certainly correct!" Mrs. Allen sounded impressed in spite of
herself. "How could Xavia possibly know about
that specter we've seen?"

"Good question," Frank admitted. "We'd better look into it. "You've never consulted her?"

"Never . . . although I have gone to fortune-
tellers sometimes, just for the fun of seeing
whether their predictions ever come true."

Mary Allen's voice was tense with emotion. She looked frightened as she reached out to grasp her husband's hand impulsively. "Oh, Jeff! Did we make a mistake by buying Blackwing Mansion?"

"Of course not, dear. I'm sure the Hardy boys will soon find out what's going on!"

"We'll certainly try," Frank promised. Seeing that Mrs. Allen appeared on the verge of tears, he and Joe ended the conversation politely and left.

"What do you make of it?" Joe asked his brother as they drove homeward.

"Don't know yet, but I'd say our first move should be to contact Madame Xavia." Frank slowed and pointed suddenly. "Hey, look who's out with his butterfly net!"

A chunky blond youth was running through a field across the street.

"Chet Morton!" Joe chuckled. "Boy, it's always something new with good old Chester! What's this—his umpty-ninth new fad?"

Chet, a teammate on the Bayport High football team and one of the Hardys' closest friends, seemed to have a new hobby every few weeks but lost interest in each almost as quickly as the mania had seized him in the first place. The Hardys yelled out to him but could not attract his attention, so they drove on.

As they walked in the front door, their tall, bony Aunt Gertrude greeted them in her usual sharp-tongued manner. "You boys had two calls while you were out gallivanting around."

"Who from, Aunty?" Frank inquired.

"One was from Chet Morton. He says to tell you he knows how you can make a lot of money."

"I'll bet!" Frank grinned at Joe. "Who else?"

"Your father called over the radio. He didn't see fit to tell me what it was all about," Miss Hardy said with a sniff, "but he wanted you to get back to him soonest—using your code scrambler."

"Wow! Then it must be important, and top secret!" Joe declared.

The boys hurried eagerly to their crime lab over the garage, where they had set up ham radio equipment. They knew their father was on the West Coast on an important government assignment, but they had no details of the case he was working on.

Frank tuned the set and beamed out the usual code. Fenton Hardy's voice soon responded.

"*FH here. Good to hear your voice, son!*"

"Dad! Where are you calling from—California?"

"No, right here in Bayport."

Both boys were startled. "Then how come you aren't home?" Joe asked.

"I'll explain later. A dangerous situation has developed, so I thought it wisest to stay undercover until—" His voice broke off.

"Dad, are you there?" Joe exclaimed, then added, "H2 calling FH—come in, please!"

There was no response.

2 A Tough Safecracker

The Hardy boys looked at each other uneasily, both unwilling to put their thoughts into words. Although this was by no means the first time a radio conversation with their father had been interrupted, the present circumstances made his sudden silence worrisome.

They had been receiving his broadcast loud and clear, and if he was in Bayport, the short sending range made it highly unlikely that sunspots could account for the interruption. So why had his transmission suddenly ended?

"If anything violent had happened, we'd have heard a noise," Frank said at length.

Joe nodded. "That's true. It's more likely he switched off his transceiver. But I'd sure like to know why!"

"So would I. Maybe he saw someone coming whom he didn't want eavesdropping on the conversation."

The boys continued trying to contact their father for another ten or fifteen minutes, hoping he might resume his transmission, but to no avail.

When they finally headed back to the house for lunch in response to Aunt Gertrude's shrill summons, Frank said, "Look, Joe. Let's not say anything about this to Mom or Aunt Gertie. No sense worrying them needlessly."

"Understood."

Their slim, attractive mother, Laura Hardy, and her unmarried sister-in-law, Gertrude, joined the two boys at the lunch table.

"Hmph," said Miss Hardy when her nephews showed no sign of reporting on their radio conversation with their father. "I suppose whatever Fenton had to tell you was too secret and confidential for our humble ears."

As she spoke, their sharp-eyed aunt gave the boys a piercing stare through her gold-rimmed glasses. Despite her scolding manner and her frequently expressed worry over the dangers of detective work, Frank and Joe knew that she enjoyed hearing about their cases. She liked nothing better than the thrill of taking part, even though it was indirectly, in the risky process of hunting down criminals and guilty parties. Her advice and suggestions were shrewd and often helpful in solving the mysteries.

"What Dad had to tell us wasn't exactly top secret, Aunt Gertrude," Joe said with a straight face, "but he did say it would be better not to discuss it with any unauthorized persons."

"Now, Joe," Mrs. Hardy said with a gently reproving glance, "stop teasing your aunt."

"Hmph," Miss Hardy exclaimed with a sniff. "Laura, if that scamp son of yours thinks I'm the least bit interested in whatever new case he, his brother and Fenton may be working on, he has another think coming!"

"I'm sorry, Aunty," said Joe. "By the way, could I please have another slice of your meat pie?"

"Well . . . I'll consider it," Miss Hardy replied, her glance softening. "Hand me your plate." Frank and Joe avidly enjoyed her mouth-watering cooking and considered her the best cake and pie-maker in Bayport. She, in turn, basked in their appreciation of her culinary skill.

"We got involved in a spooky mystery case this morning, Aunt Gertrude," Frank said, changing the subject to avoid any further talk of their father. "Do you know the old Blackwing Mansion?"

"Of course I know it. I've lived in Bayport longer than you and your brother, in case you weren't aware of that fact. You might almost say the Blackwing house is something of a town landmark. Are you going to tell me the place is haunted?"

"That's what the present owners want us to find out." Frank described the young detectives' visit to the Allens and their strange account of a weird black object hovering over the mansion at night.

"Hmph. Sounds to me like someone's nasty idea of a practical joke." Miss Hardy pursed her lips and frowned thoughtfully as she raised her teacup. "Do you know, I recall reading something about that house not long ago."

"If you could tell us where, Aunty, we'd look it up. It might give us a clue," Joe said.

"It seems to have slipped my mind just now, but I'll try to remember."

"While you're at it," Joe went on, "do you

17

recall ever hearing about a fortune-teller named Madame Xavia?"

"Indeed I have. They say she's quite good, or at least a cut above the average Gypsy palmist or tea-leaf reader."

Mrs. Hardy nodded. "Yes, I've heard the same. She's a shrewd judge of character, no doubt, but several of my friends who've gone to her think she has a genuine streak of ESP. How does she come into the picture, Joe? Have the Allens consulted her?"

"No, but she probably wants them to." Joe told his mother and aunt about the startling special-delivery letter Mr. and Mrs. Allen had received. "We'll go see Madame Xavia this afternoon," he added.

After lunch, the Hardys decided first to return Chet Morton's call. Joe dialed his number. As he had hoped, Chet's sister Iola, who was Joe's favorite girlfriend, answered.

"I'm afraid you're out of luck. Chet's still out chasing butterflies," Iola said. "But I'm glad you called."

"So am I," Joe said, smiling into the phone.

"No, seriously, a bunch of the girls are arranging a beach party at Silver Cove on Thursday night. Want to come?"

"Need you ask?"

"How do I know?" said Iola coyly.

"Well, of course I'll come! Savage beasts couldn't keep me away!"

"Don't worry, I don't think there'll be any on the beach—except for a few wolves, maybe. Anyhow, I'm glad you're coming. And tell Frank that Callie Shaw's counting on him, too."

"In that case I guarantee he'll be there."

After passing the news about the beach party to Frank, who had been looking up Madame Xavia's name in the telephone directory, Joe surrendered the phone to his brother and let him dial the psychic's number.

A recorded voice spoke from an answering machine. *"Madame Xavia is now in trance, focusing her psychic powers on the problems of someone who has come to seek her help. If you wish to consult her professionally, please listen for the signal tone, then leave your name and number, and she will respond as soon as possible. Thank you."*

The voice was that of a woman. It sounded pleasantly deep and soothing. Without waiting for the beep, Frank hung up.

Joe shot him a quizzical glance. "Aren't you going to leave a message?"

19

"No. Something tells me it may be better to walk in on her without warning."

The boys had barely turned away from the hall phone when the doorbell rang. A tall, sandy-haired man stood on the front porch.

"Hi, Sam," said Joe after opening the door. "Come on in."

Sam Radley was a skilled detective, their father's most reliable operative. His quiet, pleasant appearance was deceptive, masking a tough, cool-nerved manhunter. It gave him perfect cover on any shadowing job.

"What's up?" Frank asked, noticing Sam's troubled frown.

"Can we talk privately somewhere, Frank?"

"Sure, come into Dad's office." The famed investigator's study was kept locked when he was away on assignment, but he always left a key with his sons, in case they needed to consult his crime files.

Frank unlocked the door. Radley and the two Hardys went inside and found chairs.

"I spoke to your dad this morning," Sam began. "He's here in Bayport. Did you know?"

"Yes, we had a call from him, too," Joe said, "but we never found out what it was about."

Radley looked worried when he heard how

20

Fenton Hardy's transmission had broken off abruptly. "That may tie in with what he was telling me." The detective explained that Mr. Hardy had warned him to watch out for a crook named Ranse Hobb. "So I thought I'd better come here and see what we can find on him in your dad's files," he concluded.

"Let's take a look," Frank said, rising from his chair.

A search of the file drawer labeled "H" quickly revealed "mug shots" of Hobb and a resumé of his lengthy criminal record.

"Tough-looking hood, isn't he!" Joe muttered.

Sam Radley nodded grimly. "Yes, and plenty dangerous, judging by his past."

Though he had been indicted a number of times, for crimes ranging from armed robbery to assault, Hobb had been convicted only once—on evidence provided by Fenton Hardy. His police record indicated that he had begun as a petty thief, gone on to expert burglary and safecracking and then to crimes of violence. A penciled note in Mr. Hardy's handwriting also mentioned an FBI suspicion that Ranse Hobb might have mob connections.

"Any idea why Dad warned you to watch out for him?" Frank queried.

21

"No, but I've had a couple of mysterious phone calls lately," Radley replied.

"What about?"

"Telling me to urge your dad to lay off his present case and advising me not to accept any assignments from him if I want to stay healthy."

Joe gave a low whistle. "What are you going to do, Sam?"

"Keep my eyes and ears open. And I think you fellows should do likewise."

Soon after Radley left, the Hardy boys drove to Madame Xavia's address—a curtained storefront office near the Bayport business district. They waited in an incense-scented reception room for about ten minutes. Then an inner door opened and a tall, purple-gowned woman with graying, shoulder-length hair—evidently Madame Xavia herself—beckoned them into her private sanctum.

"Please be seated. You have come without an appointment."

"Yes," said Frank. "We're here for an urg—"

"Silence!" She raised her hand, then touched her fingertips to her temples and closed her eyes. "You are clever young men. You investigate mysteries, I think, and have solved many."

Joe shot a glance at his brother, who merely

22

shrugged and said, "If you see that much, Madame Xavia, what can you tell us about Mr. and Mrs. Allen at Blackwing Mansion?"

The psychic gasped. "I fear the dark cloud over their house may conceal the *Angel of Death*!"

3   *A Ghostly Voice*

Madame Xavia's sudden change of manner caught the Hardy boys by surprise. She seemed genuinely frightened by whatever mental vision she was seeing or sensing behind her closed eyelids.

"What dark cloud are you talking about, Madame Xavia?" Frank demanded sharply.

"It is something I have already warned the Allens about by letter." She spoke in a hollow, ominous, trancelike tone.

"We know about that letter," Joe said. "But you still haven't answered my brother's question. And you've never even met the Allens. So what's all this about a dark cloud hanging over their house?"

"It is not necessary for me to have met someone to sense a danger that may be threatening that person!"

"Oh, come on now," Frank challenged scornfully, deliberately goading her. "Most psychics at least have to touch something belonging to a person before they can pick up any vibrations. Why should you sense anything at all about the Allens? You have nothing to do with the Blackwing Mansion . . . or have you?"

Madame Xavia's hands came slowly away from her forehead. They seemed to be trembling. She opened her eyes, then blinked rapidly, appearing to come out of her trance into the light of day. "I have nothing more to tell you," she intoned.

"But your letter to the Allens said you'd be glad to help them with any advice you could offer," Joe persisted.

"That offer applies to the Allens alone. If *they* wish to consult me, perhaps their psychic auras may enable me to perceive more clearly what fate holds in store." The fortuneteller's skin was clammy with perspiration, and her eyes seemed to have sunk more deeply into their sockets as she added, "Why should I waste breath on un-believing skeptics like you two?"

"We're here on behalf of the Allens," Frank pointed out. "They've asked us to try and solve the mystery of the Blackwing Mansion."

Madame Xavia drew herself up to her full, imposing, purple-gowned height. She looked like a gaunt witch casting a spell. "I have nothing more to say," she declared. "Kindly leave my consulting room at once!"

The Hardys had no choice except to walk out of her storefront office. "Whew! What a weirdo!" Joe muttered once they were outside. "But she seemed to know all about us."

"That's not surprising," Frank said. "Dad's made the Hardy name famous, and you and I've been interviewed on TV and had our pictures in the paper half a dozen times."

"True, but she still clued in pretty fast." As they drove away, Joe went on. "I've a hunch she knows more than she let on about whatever's haunting the Blackwing Mansion."

Frank nodded thoughtfully. "I agree. She was definitely holding out on us . . . and she sure looked spooked about something. Maybe what-ever's haunting the mansion has her scared out of her wits."

On their way home to Elm Street, the Hardys decided to stop at the Morton farmhouse to see if Chet had returned from his butterfly-hunting expedition.

As they pulled into the rutted drive, they saw their plump pal tiptoeing toward some bushes bordering the vegetable patch. When Chet caught sight of them, he put his finger to his lips and waggled his hand, gesturing to them not to make any loud noise or sudden disturbance. A butterfly net was poised in his other hand.

"Good grief, what's he after now?" Joe murmured under his breath.

The Hardys hurried to join their friend. He pointed to a huge winged beauty clinging to a branch of the shrubbery. It was gorgeously marked in red, orange, yellow and brown, with black streaks and silvery-white spots.

"Tony Prito came by a while ago and told me it was out here, but I didn't believe him," Chet whispered. "Then I spotted it myself out the window while I was having lunch. It's a great spangled fritillary, I think!"

"A great spangled what?" said Joe.

"Fritillary."

"You sure you know what you're talking about?"

"Sure, I'm sure," snapped Chet. "You think I don't know a fritillary when I see one? And man, this one's humongous! It could make butterfly history! . . . Now pipe down while I snag it!"

He inched closer, then lashed out with his net in a lightning-quick downward swoop. As the branch broke, there was a loud explosion, followed by a shower of soot from a tree limb overhead. Chet gaped at the Hardys in sudden black-faced dismay!

Frank and Joe burst into helpless laughter. A trip wire from the bush had obviously triggered a carefully rigged cherry bomb and tipped over a plastic pail full of soot that had been precariously balanced on the tree branch. The fake butterfly was still glued to the broken-off twig.

Black-haired Tony Prito and lanky Biff Hooper suddenly rose into view from behind the clump of bushes.

"What was that you were saying about a great spangled huckleberry, professor?" Biff asked, trying in vain to keep from grinning.

Chet's moon face contorted in sudden rage. "All right, you wise guys!" he yelled. "I'll get you for this!" Dropping his butterfly net, he charged after the two pranksters.

When he was aroused to fighting fury, the

beefy youth made a formidable foe. Biff and Tony, who were shaking with laughter, were in no shape to withstand his attack.

A wild chase ensued around the vegetable patch and through the barnyard, climaxed by a rolling, pummeling free-for-all while Frank and Joe looked on, cheering and howling with glee.

The battle ended when Iola, a cute sixteen-year-old with dark ringleted hair, made peace by bringing out a pitcher of iced lemonade, paper cups and a damp washcloth for Chet to wipe his face with. Her good-natured, roly-poly brother was soon chuckling at the memory of his own discomfiture when he had tried to snare the booby-trapped butterfly.

"What's this big money-making scheme you told Aunt Gertie about?" Joe asked him.

"Listen, it's on the level!" declared Chet, turning serious. "How'd you two guys like to earn five thousand bucks?"

"Doing what? Peddling gilded butterflies?"

"No, I'm serious. All you have to do is find a valuable butterfly specimen that was stolen from a rich collector named Drexel. He lives right here in Bayport. That's how big a reward he's offering!"

Frank and Joe glanced at each other in surprise. This was a good deal different from Chet's usual fantastic get-rich-quick schemes.

"Hmm . . . sounds interesting," said Frank. "But we'll have to think it over."

"Right," Joe agreed. "We don't usually go out drumming up business or trying to collect rewards."

"And we don't know beans about butterflies," Frank added.

"Never mind all that. This is a straight crime-solving job, right up your alley. At least think about it, okay?"

"Okay, that much we can promise."

When the Hardy boys arrived home, they came in through the kitchen door. Aunt Gertrude was just pulling a tray of delicious-smelling oatmeal cookies out of the oven.

"Talked to that psychic woman, did you?" she inquired.

"Yes," said Frank, "but we didn't learn much."

"Hmph. Probably didn't go about it the right way. What did she have to say for herself?"

"We'll tell you all about it, Aunty," Joe said with a wink at his brother, "if you'll let us have a couple of those cookies."

Miss Hardy frowned severely at her younger

nephew through her gold-rimmed spectacles. Then her sharp-featured face softened to a smile. "Well . . . I might consider it. But don't go spoiling your appetite for dinner."

Presently the two boys were seated at the kitchen table with a plateful of fresh cookies between them. Frank related their conversation with Madame Xavia, while Joe threw in additional details from time to time as he munched.

"So you think she knows more than she's telling?" Miss Hardy said.

Frank nodded. "I'm sure of it, Aunt Gertrude."

"Hmph." Miss Hardy pursed her lips, and a steely glint came into her eyes. "Perhaps I should go and talk to this Madame Xavia."

"Would you, Aunty?" Joe exclaimed.

"Why not? Maybe she'll find it easier to talk to another woman. In any case, I'll stand for no nonsense. If I conclude that she does know something about the trouble the Allens are having, she'll either tell me all about it or I'll know the reason why she's holding out."

Frank and Joe glanced at each other with slightly awed grins. Having said that she would make Madame Xavia talk, there was not much doubt in either of their minds that their aunt would make good on her promise.

With no homework to do during summer vacation, the two boys spent a lazy evening, and after their mother and Aunt Gertrude had gone to bed, they sat up watching a late TV show. Both were startled when the telephone rang.

"Maybe it's Sam Radley—or Dad!" Joe said. He got to the front hall before Frank and picked up the phone. The caller was Jeff Allen.

"Could you fellows come over right away?"

"Sure," Joe said. "Something wrong?"

"It's Captain Blackwing again! Can't you hear him?"

Joe turned the receiver slightly for Frank to listen in, too. A deep, hoarse voice could be heard in the background, bellowing nautical commands and curses.

"Lay aloft, you lubbers, and shake out that canvas double quick! Look smart there, boyo, or I'll have the bosun stripe your back! If that patrol cutter catches us with this black cargo, we could all wind up in irons—or dangling from a Limey yardarm!"

"Oh, no!" Joe cried. "It *is* Captain Blackwing! We'll be right over!"

The Hardys hurried outside and went whizzing off in their yellow sports car. The moon was bright and nearly full. As they reached Indian Road and approached the Allens' house, Frank gasped. "Look there, Joe! Just ahead!"

A black-winged creature could be seen, clearly silhouetted in the moonlight, as it soared above the treetops!

4 Midnight Meeting

The boys were speechless as they stared at the weird spectacle. A moment later, it was lost to view through their windshield. Joe stuck his head out the car window, hoping to glimpse it again. However, the flying black demon was no longer visible in the starry darkness overhead.

"Wow!" Joe murmured in awe. "I'm not sure I believe my own eyes!"

"We saw it, all right!" Frank declared grimly. He swung up the drive between the stone gateposts, slammed on the brakes, and both boys leaped out of the car.

Jeff Allen was standing on the porch steps of the mansion. "Did you get a look at that thing swooping over the house?" he called to the Hardys.

"Yes, we glimpsed it as we were driving up," Joe said, "and we sure understand now why you and your wife don't like it!"

"Mary's pretty badly shaken, I'm afraid," Jeff told them as he brought the boys inside.

Mrs. Allen was waiting, as before, in the living room, looking pale and distraught. Her husband put a comforting arm around her shoulders.

"The two of you heard the ghost voice first, is that right?" Frank asked.

"Yes, that's nearly always how it happens," Jeff Allen confirmed. "Captain Blackwing begins speaking, and then pretty soon if we look out the window we can see that horrible black monster flitting around over the house."

"The voice wasn't the only thing we heard," Mrs. Allen added.

"What else?"

"Thumps on the roof, as if the captain was up there, clumping around in his sea boots on the widow's walk."

The Hardys knew that the term "widow's walk" referred to a flat, railed-in roof area, and that such a feature was often found on New England houses built by whaling skippers and other seafaring men. Supposedly their wives paced about on these roof walks, gazing out to sea as they waited and watched for their husbands' ship to return.

"Is tonight the first time you've heard him up there?" Frank went on.

"Oh, no, it's happened several times before . . . but not nearly as often as we've heard the ghost talking," Mary replied.

"If anything solid enough to make thumping noises has been up on your roof," Joe put in, "it may have left a clue."

"Right," Frank agreed. "We'll come back tomorrow morning and look around in the daylight, if that's okay with you."

"Please do, by all means," Jeff Allen urged. "Anything you can do to clear up this ghastly business will be appreciated."

The boys drove home soon afterward and parked in the garage. As they got out, they heard a loud alarm buzzer go off and keep ringing on the second floor.

"It's the radio! A transmission's coming in!" Joe exclaimed. "Maybe Dad's trying to contact us again!"

He and Frank hurried up to their crime lab. Joe's hunch proved correct. Their father's voice was soon coming over the speaker. "Sorry I had to break off last time, fellows, but someone almost trapped me in the place where I'd set up my transceiver, so I had to clear out fast."

"Thank goodness you're safe, Dad—that's all that matters!" Frank responded. "Sure is a relief to hear from you!"

"I'd like to fill you two in on my current case, but not over the air—even with a scrambler," Fenton Hardy continued. "This place I'm transmitting from right now isn't much more secure than the last one. I'd prefer we meet face-to-face."

"You name it and we'll be there, Dad," said Joe. "Where did you have in mind?"

"Out on Barmet Bay might be safest. That'll make it harder for any sneak to eavesdrop or to maneuver us into a trap. But don't take the *Sleuth* if you can find another boat. There's always a risk someone may be keeping a watch on our boathouse."

Frank said, "Maybe we can borrow Tony Prito's *Napoli*."

"Good! Do that if you can." Mr. Hardy described a place on the bay for their meeting, then signed off.

Rather than phone and possibly wake up the whole Prito family at this late hour, the boys immediately backed their car out of the garage and sped to Tony's house. They were prepared to toss pebbles at his bedroom window, but a light was on in the living room. It turned out that Tony was still up watching TV.

"Sure," their friend agreed readily when they asked to borrow his boat. "I wouldn't mind going with you if I didn't have to help out Dad on a construction job early tomorrow morning. Wait'll I get you the keys."

It was nearing midnight when the Hardys gently putt-putted out of the marina slip where the *Napoli* had been berthed. The bay was glassy except for occasional smooth, oily swells, and the moon laid a broad band of silver across the water.

Gradually they picked up speed and were soon planing out of the harbor toward the southern headland of the bay, where the meeting was to take place. The dense shadow cast by the headland would provide ample cover of darkness for their rendezvous.

The repeated calls of a nightbird reached their ears, each time followed by a low whistle. These were the agreed-upon signals, and presently a few discreet beams from a flashlight enabled them to steer alongside their father's boat.

"How are you, my boys?" Fenton Hardy greeted them warmly, reaching out to give each of his sons a quick hug and handclasp.

"Sure is good to see you, Dad," Joe said, returning the embrace. "What's this case all about?"

Mr. Hardy explained that during the past year a number of industrial plants all around the country had been hit by daring thefts. The companies involved were hi-tech firms, mostly engaged in computer and electronics work, often with important defense contracts. The thief seemed able to get past guard dogs, security fences and burglar alarms with little or no difficulty.

"Do you think some enemy spy ring is behind the robberies?" Frank asked.

"Not necessarily, but there's not much doubt a lot of the stuff gets sold to foreign buyers. Almost all of it's restricted from export," Mr. Hardy replied.

"Any suspects?" Joe inquired.

The master sleuth frowned and rubbed his jaw. "To be honest, we've no real clues yet.

But both the FBI and the CIA have a hunch the jobs are being masterminded by a slick international crook and arms dealer named Klaus Kane."

In the past, Mr. Hardy told the boys, Kane had often employed the safecracker and strong-arm man Ranse Hobb in his American operations.

"That's why you warned Sam Radley to watch out for him?" Joe queried.

"Right. Hobb's been traced to the vicinity of Bayport—and the FBI's had a tip that Kane may be headed this way, too. That's why I've been trying to keep my presence here a secret. If it leaks out that I'm working on this case, it may attract attention to our house and put the whole family in danger. But now it looks very much as if the enemy's clued in despite my precautions."

"It sure does," said Frank. "Sam Radley's already received phone threats."

Before Mr. Hardy could reply, a faint sound reached their ears across the water. In the darkness, it was impossible to make out the source, but all three Hardys immediately froze.

"Someone's out there." Joe hissed softly.

"You boys get back to Bayport right away," their father ordered. "I'll handle this!" Frank and Joe started to protest but were curtly warned to silence. Reluctantly, they keyed the *Napoli's* engine to life and started back toward the harbor.

Moments later, as they sped across the bay, the darkness was pierced by a sudden bright flash, then a sharp explosion!

5 Boathouse Ploy

The blast sent ominous echoes rolling across the bay, and a thrill of alarm raced through the Hardy boys.

Joe shot a frightened glance at his brother.

"We'd better go back and check on Dad!"

Instead, Frank throttled the *Napoli* and brought the boat to a halt. He turned off the noisy engine and listened. In the distance, the boys could hear the distinct sounds of two motorboats going in different directions.

"Dad's all right," Frank said. "The grenade or whatever it was did not hit him."

Joe let out a sigh of relief as his brother started

the engine again. A moment later, they were on their way to shore.

The Hardys' boathouse was clearly discernible in the moonlight as they entered the harbor. Gazing at it, Frank thought he detected someone or something moving in the shadows. He picked up the night glasses they had brought along and focused on the source of the movement.

"Joe!" he hissed a moment later. "Take a look at the boathouse!" He passed the binoculars to his brother.

"Oh, oh!" Joe muttered as he peered through the glasses. "Someone's tampering with the door lock!"

They were heading toward the marina, but Frank, who was piloting the *Napoli*, now veered toward the boathouse for a closer look.

There was no way to muffle the noise of their engine. As they approached, a shadowy figure suddenly broke away from the small building and dashed off into the darkness.

"There he goes!" said Joe through gritted teeth. But both Hardys realized it was hopeless to go after the prowler. By the time they pulled up to the dock, made fast to a bollard and scrambled in pursuit, their unknown enemy would be out of sight and out of reach.

"Well, at least we scared him off before he had time to break in," Joe remarked glumly.

"Don't be too sure of that," said Frank.

"Meaning what?"

"Maybe he already broke in before we spotted him."

Joe glanced sharply at his brother. "Then what was he doing monkeying at the door?"

"Good question. Maybe we'd better find out." Turning the wheel over to Joe, Frank stripped quickly to his shorts. Then he eased himself over the side, taking with him a waterproof flashlight from the boat's locker.

The water was chilly and dark. Frank dived downward, cleaving his way with smooth, powerful strokes, and came up inside the boathouse, just abeam of the Hardys' own motorboat, the *Sleuth*.

Pulling himself up onto the walkway, Frank thumbed the flashlight and played its beam around the walls, fearing the intruder might have tampered somehow with the light switch.

There was no sign of any such sabotage. But Frank caught his breath as he saw something wired to the inside door handle.

Ten minutes later he emerged, grim-faced, alongside *Napoli* and climbed aboard.

44

"What did you find?" Joe asked.

"The door was booby-trapped—with a Molotov cocktail!"

Joe gulped and shuddered as Frank described the horrifying setup. A bottle of gasoline, stoppered with a rag, had been rigged over the doorway. Turning the door handle on the outside would have triggered a spark to ignite the wick, and when the door was pushed open, the blazing firebomb would have been pulled straight down on the head of the person who entered.

Not only would the victim have been set afire, but the whole boathouse would doubtlessly have burned to the water!

"Any creep who'd do that," Joe declared, "belongs behind bars!"

"Right," Frank agreed. "Let's hope Dad puts him there!"

The remark reminded both boys of the peril their father had faced out on the bay in the inky shadow of the headland. How soon, they wondered, would they know his whereabouts?

Frank dried himself as best he could and pulled on his clothes. Then the Hardys berthed the *Napoli* in its marina slip and headed homeward through the moonlit darkness in their yellow sports sedan, stopping only long enough en route to deposit the boat's keys in the Pritos' mailbox, as prearranged with Tony.

At breakfast the next morning Aunt Gertrude eyed her two nephews quizzically as she heaped their plates with bacon and eggs. "Did I hear you two go out gallivanting somewhere last night?"

Frank smiled. "That's right, Aunty. We, er, had an emergency call from the Allens." He thought it wisest not to mention the meeting with their father on Barmet Bay or the deadly booby trap set by the boathouse intruder.

"I gather the Allens had another visit from that Blackwing ghost?" Miss Hardy demanded.

"They sure did," said Joe, pitching into his food. "And we saw it! We even heard Captain Blackwing's voice!"

Their aunt settled down at the table to listen to their story, frowning over her gold-rimmed glasses and pursing her lips suspiciously. "That flying black creature," she commented. "It couldn't by any chance be a bird-shaped balloon, could it? Or some kind of miniature dirigible?"

"Sounds pretty far out, but that's as good a guess as anything I can come up with," Frank admitted. "If you're right, though, who's piloting the thing?"

"Hmph! Someone who's trying to scare that poor young couple out of their wits," Miss Hardy retorted.

"I'll buy that," Joe agreed. "Mrs. Allen said they also heard the ghost clumping around up on the roof in his sea boots."

Gertrude Hardy gave a scornful sniff. "Ghosts in sea boots, indeed!"

"Well, I don't know of any squirrels who wear sea boots," Joe said innocently. "And it wasn't hailing last night, either. So what made the noises?"

"Hmph!" Miss Hardy rose from the table, teacup and saucer in hand. "You two and Fenton are supposed to be the detectives in this family. Find out!"

Frank chuckled. "We intend to, Aunt Gertrude!"

Ten minutes later the Hardy boys were on their way to Indian Road. When they arrived at Blackwing Mansion, Jeff and Mary Allen still looked somewhat haggard from the previous night's spooky manifestations.

"We'd like to take a look on the widow's walk," Frank told them.

"Good. I was about to go up there myself," said Jeff. "Just follow me, boys."

He led the way up a spiral staircase to a small door in the tower, which opened directly onto the flat roof area. The Hardys paced about, not only examining the surface of the widow's walk for traces of a ghostly visitor but gazing out in all directions.

The view from atop the high old Victorian mansion was magnificent. The house was backed against a hillside. But to the east, beyond the trees, the boys could glimpse the blue, sun-glinting waters of Barmet Bay, dotted here and there with white sails.

Neither of the Hardys, however, could find any sign of whatever had made the clumping sounds.

"*Something* was up here last night," Jeff Allen declared stubbornly. "I'm sure of that."

Frank nodded. "We don't doubt it. The biggest question, though, is how to explain that black-winged specter."

"You fellows saw that yourselves. I don't have to convince you it's not just a figment of my imagination!"

Frank nodded thoughtfully. "You've spoken of

the thing *hovering* over your house. Do you mean that sometimes it just hangs up in the air without moving?"

"No, it . . . well, it circles around . . . like a hunting hawk that's scanning for prey, just before it swoops."

"You mentioned before that it casts a shadow," Joe cut in.

"Yes, as a matter of fact, it does," Jeff Allen replied. "I remember one night I happened to glance out the window and saw a big black shadow in the moonlight, as if a giant bird was winging overhead. So I ran outside and looked up at the sky—and sure enough, it was the Blackwing ghost."

"Well, then, if it casts a shadow, it *must* be real," Joe said with a dry grin. "A glider, perhaps?"

"But a glider couldn't just circle or hover over the house," Frank pointed out, then glanced at Jeff Allen again. "Does it make any noise?"

Allen shook his head. "None . . . or at least none that we can hear. That's part of what makes it so spooky and weird, seeing it fly around in total silence."

"Which means it can't be a powered aircraft,

either. So if it's real, Joe, how do we explain what's keeping it up there?"

"Search me." The younger Hardy boy shrugged. "Maybe Aunt Gertie has something with her balloon theory. But look, Frank, if anybody *was* clumping around on the roof last night, there's how he must have climbed up." Joe pointed to the nearest overhanging tree.

"That figures." Frank nodded. "Assuming it's possible to climb that particular tree."

"I'll soon find out!" Joe hurried downstairs and outside.

The big, broad-spreading hickory had branches low enough for him to grab one and swing himself up. Once he had gained a secure foothold, he was able to ascend rapidly. In a few minutes he reached rooftop height, and he began groping his way out on the stout branch that overhung the mansion.

Frank and Mr. Allen were watching his progress intently. "Were there any scratch marks that might tell us if anyone climbed the tree recently?" Frank called.

"I didn't notice any," Joe replied, "though of course the intruder may have been wearing rubber-soled shoes."

He was almost close enough now to jump

down onto the widow's walk, when he paused suddenly with a muttered gasp. "Oh, oh—!"

A bright metallic object was caught in the leafy branches just a few feet away!

6   *African Clue*

"What's the matter?" Jeff Allen queried, noticing Joe's reaction.

Joe pointed to the shiny object that had caught his eye. "Looks like your visitor may have lost something."

He squirmed a bit farther along the branch until he could reach out and snatch the object. Then, almost in the same agile maneuver, Joe swung himself down onto the widow's walk.

"What did you find?" Frank asked eagerly.

"A butterfly, believe it or not!" Joe held it out for his brother and Mr. Allen to see.

The metal object—evidently an ornament of

some kind—appeared to be made of silver, with the butterfly's wings enameled in brilliant colors of iridescent blue and gold. Attached to either forewing was a length of delicate silver chain, ending in a broken link.

"Looks as though it was torn off when the person who was wearing it jumped onto the roof," Jeff Allen suggested.

"Right," Joe agreed. "It probably got caught on a twig of the tree branch. Maybe our ghost didn't even realize he'd lost it—or if he did, he had no way to find it again in the dark."

To prove that the intruder could have gotten down from the roof the same way he climbed up, Joe tugged on the overhanging branch until he got a good grip, then swung himself into the boughs and shinnied down the trunk even faster than his upward climb.

Mary Allen was fascinated when the young detective showed her the beautiful ornament. Like her husband, she had never seen it before and could offer no explanation of how it got snagged in the tree, except that their spooky tormentor must have lost it during one of his nocturnal visits.

"He probably wore it either as a necklace or bracelet," Joe guessed. From the length of chain still attached, a necklace seemed more likely.

"One thing's certain," Frank declared. "Ghosts don't wear ornaments that get ripped off, any more than they clump around on roofs. I'd call this conclusive evidence that someone's just playing a dirty trick on you folks."

"Can you think of anyone who might want to scare you away from here?" Joe asked.

Jeff and Mary Allen looked at each other, and Jeff grinned wryly. "Well, we seem to get along with our neighbors okay—but as a matter of fact, yes, I can think of two or three people who might fit into that category."

Frank said, "Mind telling us who they are?"

"Well, if you want a complete list, I suppose I should start at the beginning. We bought this house about a year ago. It was in pretty bad shape and needed a lot of work. But almost as soon as we began restoring it, a buyer showed up who wanted to take it off our hands—even though the house had been standing vacant for years before we saw it."

Mrs. Allen smiled reminiscently. "He was really eager. I guess he saw the same possibilities in this place that we did. He offered us an excellent price! But of course we turned him down."

"Do you remember who he was?" Frank asked.

Jeff Allen frowned and pinched his lip thoughtfully. "Somebody from out of town who just happened to be passing through, as I recall . . . hanged if I can remember his name, though." He shot another glance at his wife. "Can you remember it, Mary?"

She shook her head. "I'm afraid not. We only saw him once—and then he phoned back that same evening, hoping we might have changed our minds. He seemed perfectly nice, though . . . unlike some of the other people who have been at us to sell."

"Who are they?" Joe asked.

"Well, one is the realtor who sold us the house," Mr. Allen replied. "His name's Jonas Milgrim. He has an office on Sycamore Street. Originally he acted as agent for the previous owners, or their estate; they moved away or died some time ago. But then just a couple of months after we purchased the place, Milgrim tried to buy it back."

"Did he say why?"

"Oh, first he gave us a big buildup about finding a much more desirable property that we'd like a lot better. He said he could arrange a trade that would earn us ten thousand dollars in value."

"And when we said no thanks," Mary Allen added, "he turned nasty."

Jeff nodded grimly. "He sure did. He caused us all sorts of legal trouble, trying to have the court declare that our deed to the house was no good on some quibbling little legal technicality. And then, as if that weren't enough of a nuisance, a guy named Clyde Peachum came along and started nagging us to sell."

"Who's he?" Frank inquired.

"A big-shot financier and real-estate developer. He tried all sorts of ways to get us to sell, first coaxing us and then threatening us. But I told him to get lost," Jeff Allen ended.

The Hardys felt that both Milgrim and Peachum were worth investigating. But as they drove away from the Blackwing Mansion, Joe proposed that first they see what they could find out about the butterfly ornament.

"It looks handmade to me," he said. "If we can learn where it came from, it may give us a lead on whoever's trying to frighten the Allens."

"Good idea," Frank agreed. "What about Arnheim's Jewelry Shop downtown? Mr. Arnheim does a lot of craftwork himself. Besides, we helped him solve a mystery once."

"Just the guy I was thinking of."

Mr. Arnheim was a skilled gold- and silver-smith who had learned his trade in Europe and had then come to America to open his own business. "Hmm, fascinating," he murmured as he examined the butterfly ornament. "Beautiful workmanship!"

"Handmade?" Joe inquired.

"Of course! Absolutely!" The jeweler's tone sounded almost scornful of such a question. "Work of this quality could never be created by a machine!"

"Any chance this could have been made by an American Indian? The Navahos are fine silver craftsmen, aren't they?"

"True, and there are expert silver artisans in Mexico, as well. But I am almost certain this was not made anywhere in the Americas." Mr. Arnheim frowned, then screwed a jeweler's glass into one eye for an even closer study of the ornament. "No, this is definitely Moorish workmanship. I would say it comes from one of the Arab countries of North Africa—Egypt, perhaps, or more likely Morocco."

The Hardys thanked Mr. Arnheim and left his store. Both of them were thoughtful.

"Captain Blackwing was a slaver, and this comes from Africa," Joe mused as they drove home. "Do you think there's any connection, Frank?"

His brother shrugged. "Sounds pretty far-fetched, but at this point I wouldn't count out *any* theory!"

Over lunch Aunt Gertrude announced that she had made an appointment by phone for a consultation that afternoon with the psychic adviser, Madame Xavia.

"Did you speak with her personally?" Frank asked.

"Of course! Do you think I would deal with just anybody?"

Frank grinned. "What did you make of her voice?"

Miss Hardy's sharp-featured face took on a shrewdly thoughtful expression. "The woman's no fool, I'll say that much. As to whether her word can be trusted, I'll decide that when I see her."

Her nephews exchanged fleeting glances, but neither smiled. They had no doubt that their aunt's opinion would be well worth waiting for.

The conversation reminded Frank and Joe about following up on the two persons who had been pressuring the Allens to sell the Blackwing Mansion.

The realtor, Jonas Milgrim, was listed in the

telephone directory. However, since his office was probably open all day to walk-in customers, the Hardys decided it might be better to confront him without warning, as they had done with Madame Xavia.

There was no individual listing in the Bayport phone book for anyone named Peachum. So Frank dialed the number of the Peachum Development Corporation. When a switchboard operator answered, he asked to speak to Mr. Peachum and was transferred to Peachum's secretary. Frank asked for an appointment.

"May I ask what you wish to see Mr. Peachum about?" the secretary inquired.

"About a piece of property he's interested in," Frank replied dryly with a wink at Joe.

"Which property is that, please?"

"Sorry," said Frank, "but this is a confidential matter we can only discuss with Mr. Peachum himself."

A haughty sniff of displeasure came over the phone. But after several moments of silence, during which she presumably consulted with her boss, the secretary informed Frank that Mr. Peachum would see the Hardy boys at three-thirty that afternoon.

Just as Frank was hanging up, a familiar voice was heard at the kitchen screen door.

59

"There's Chet Morton," Joe said, and went to let his friend in.

Chet had come to invite the Hardys to see some of his newly captured butterfly beauties, so all three piled into the boys' yellow sports car and drove to the Morton farmhouse.

To Frank and Joe's surprise, the butterflies were flitting about in a screened-in porch, where Iola and her mother raised a variety of indoor plants.

"Are you going to mount them?" Frank asked.

Chet shrugged. "Nah, Iola won't let me. She says we oughtn't kill any living creature if we can help it. Photographing them is more fun, anyhow."

The Hardys were impressed when they saw Chet's prize color shots, which included pictures of a gorgeous orange-and-black monarch, a red admiral, a great purple hairstreak that looked more bluish-green than purple, and a painted lady.

"Hey, these are really good, Chet!" Frank exclaimed.

"Not bad for an amateur naturalist," Chet said, puffing up with pleasure at Frank's praise.

Joe pulled out the butterfly ornament he had found in the tree overhanging the Blackwing Mansion. "Can you identify this, Chet?"

His roly-poly chum studied it with obvious interest. "Hmm . . . it reminds me of a mourning cloak—what the British call a Camberwell Beauty—with that gold border along the edge of the wings. But those are mostly reddish brown, not blue."

Chet paused and looked up. "If you really want to know, I could introduce you to that collector named Drexel—the guy I told you about yesterday."

"Why not?" Joe said after a questioning glance at his brother, who nodded agreement.

The three drove to the collector's home, which was located in a wealthy suburb of Bayport, and were ushered into the drawing room by a servant. Bradford Drexel himself proved to be an elderly gentleman with a gray mustache, who looked as though he had spent a good deal of time in the tropics.

On meeting the Hardy boys, his deeply tanned face lit up with eager interest. "The very chaps I wanted to see!" he exclaimed.

7 *The Drexel Caper*

"What did you want to see us about, sir?" Frank asked Mr. Drexel. "The valuable butterfly that was stolen from your collection?"

"Ah! Chester told you about that, eh? Yes, that's exactly what I had in mind." Mr. Drexel said that he had often read about the exploits of the famed manhunter Fenton Hardy and the baffling mysteries solved by his two sons, and that he had already decided to ask their help in recovering his stolen specimen.

"Just how valuable *was* the butterfly?" Joe inquired.

The elderly collector sighed and shrugged.

"It's hard to put an exact valuation on it, I'm afraid. There's no standard price list for rare butterflies, as there is, let us say, for new cars. All I can tell you is that the specimen will be almost impossible to replace, short of mounting an expedition to the East Indies to find another one."

Drexel led his young visitors to a bookcase in his study adjoining the drawing room and took down a large volume illustrated with color photographs of all sorts of butterflies and moths. He leafed through its pages and pointed to a particular photo. "Here's what the stolen specimen looked like. Its scientific name is *Cethosia myrina*."

The picture showed a large, beautiful butterfly whose wing colors were shaded delicately from purple through rose to reddish brown and orange. Its scalloped rear wing edges were patterned in gold.

"This lovely creature is found only on the island of Celebes in Indonesia," Drexel told the boys. "Suffice it to say that I'm willing to pay five thousand dollars to get back my stolen specimen—or more if necessary."

Chet Morton's blue eyes widened at this last remark. He gave a low whistle and shot a significant glance at the Hardys, as if to say, *See there! What did I tell you?*

"That's a lot of money, all right," Joe remarked. "Were any of your other butterflies stolen at the same time?"

"No, only my *Cethosia*. Let me show you where I kept it."

There were several large glass cases in the study containing numerous mounted butterflies. But instead of going to one of these, Drexel led the boys to the central hallway of his house, where other butterflies were on display. He pointed to a glass wall case that was lighted by a metal sconce.

"Every window in this house, by the way, is protected by a burglar alarm," the collector explained. "In addition, each display case is locked, and the glass covers are rather heavy. To break one would make quite a noise—and might damage the delicate wings of the specimens inside. So the burglar not only had to disconnect a burglar alarm to get in, he also had to pick the lock of this case, and I assure you it's a high-security lock."

"It sounds as if the burglar was a pro and knew exactly what he wanted," Joe declared.

"But what would he do with the butterfly after

he had it?" Frank queried. "Keep it? Or would he be able to sell it?"

"Interesting question." Bradford Drexel frowned and stroked his gray mustache. "In effect, I suppose, you're asking me if the thief might be a collector himself. . . . Hmm. . . . Well, I'd say it wouldn't be *easy* to sell a stolen rare butterfly. On the other hand, I'm sure there are collectors who'd be willing to buy and ask no questions, just as there are art collectors who are willing to buy stolen art masterpieces. Matter of fact, there's been a whole series of rare-butterfly thefts from collections all over the country in the past year or so. No doubt that *proves* there's a market for such loot."

Frank nodded. "Sure sounds that way."

"There must be a well-organized gang at work," Joe mused. "Wouldn't you agree, Frank?"

"Definitely. I'm afraid my brother and I aren't prepared to handle that big an investigation, Mr. Drexel. Right now our dad's busy on another case, but we'll tell him about the butterfly thefts next time we talk to him, if you like, and ask him to get in touch with you as soon as he can."

"Yes, please do. Meantime, I'll make a list of all the thefts I've heard about. That'll give him something to start on."

Mr. Drexel conducted the boys back into his study. Sitting down at his desk, he consulted a sheaf of news clippings and hastily jotted down the dates and locations of the various burglaries.

"By the way," Joe said when their host had finished, "can you tell us what sort of butterfly this is—or is it just a pretty design a jewelry craftsman made up?"

Drexel examined the silver ornament that Joe handed him. He looked impressed. "No, indeed! This represents a real butterfly. It's called *Prepona deiphile*—and it's quite rare, I might add. . . . My word, this is most interesting!"

Once again he took down his illustrated catalog of butterflies from the bookshelf and pointed out a picture of the *Prepona deiphile*.

"Where does it come from?" Frank asked.

"South America—or, more precisely, the mountains of southern Brazil. It's a high flier, you see. And not only high—according to some experts, the *Prepona* are the fastest-flying butterflies in the world!"

Drexel was so fascinated by the unique ornament that he offered to buy it at any price the boys cared to name. But Joe declined.

"Actually, we—uh, don't know who owns it,

sir. It turned up in connection with a mystery we're trying to solve. But when and if we find the owner, we'll tell him you'd like to buy it."

The Hardys and Chet were about to leave when the butler announced another visitor. "It's a gentleman who collects butterflies, sir. He came to see you once before—Mr. Saxby."

"Ah, yes, of course." Bradford Drexel nodded. "Show him in, please."

The newcomer proved to be a dark-haired man in his thirties with a brisk, almost nervous manner and penetrating gray-green eyes.

"Nice to see you again, Saxby," said Drexel, shaking hands. "You're in Bayport to stay awhile, I hope?"

"Only a few days. Just passing through, really. I heard you'd been robbed, so I thought I'd stop in and extend my sympathy. What did the thieves get—anything valuable?" Saxby's glance darted about the room, taking in the display cases.

"My prize specimen, I'm afraid—*Cethosia myrina.*" As a look of angry dismay passed over his visitor's face, Drexel shrugged and smiled ruefully. "But before we get into that, let me introduce my young friends."

Seeing that the two collectors wished to talk about butterflies, the Hardys and Chet stayed just long enough to chat politely for a few moments, then left.

Frank glanced at his watch as he took the wheel. "Almost time for our appointment with Peachum."

"Who's Peachum?" Chet asked.

"Some guy who's been trying to high-pressure the Allens into selling their house," Joe replied. The Hardys had already told their friend about the mystery of the Blackwing ghost. "We figure someone's probably trying to scare the Allens into moving out, and Peachum might be the nasty joker who's behind it all. Want to come along while we beard him in his den?"

"Not me!" Chet shook his head emphatically and crammed a saved-up hunk of candy bar into his mouth. "I'll leave the ghosts and nasty jokers to you two. Personally, I prefer butterflies!"

Clyde Peachum's business occupied a plush suite in a downtown office building. He was a portly, heavy-jowled man with long gray hair flowing over the back of his collar and an odor of cigar smoke clinging to his well-tailored suit. His manner was cold and suspicious, yet outwardly polite as the Hardy boys were ushered into his office. "My secretary says you have a piece of property I may be interested in," he said when they were all seated.

"No, sir, that's not quite right," Frank corrected him. "We've come to *talk* about a piece of property you're interested in."

"What property is that?"

"The Blackwing Mansion."

Peachum's eyes grew colder, and his beetling brows puckered into a scowl. "What's the angle, sonny? You two think you can talk the Allens into selling?"

"No way, Mr. Peachum," Joe said. "We've come to find out why you're so interested in buying."

"And just what makes you think that's any business of yours?"

"Our business is solving mysteries," Frank said evenly. "It's obvious someone's trying to scare the Allens away from Blackwing Mansion—and apparently you're pretty eager to get hold of the place. A lot of people might jump to the conclusion that there's a connection between those two facts. Maybe you'd care to explain."

Clyde Peachum chuckled coldly, but there was nothing humorous about the expression on his face. "You brats have really got a nerve coming in here with a line like that!" he rasped. "I have nothing to explain to you two—and if you know what's good for you, from now on you'll keep your noses out of my business!"

He punched a bell on his desk, then plucked a cigar from a humidor, bit off its tip and clamped the cigar between his teeth. As his secretary appeared in the doorway, he growled, "Show these punks out—and don't ever let them back in!"

Frank and Joe were flushed with anger, but they left in grim silence, realizing there was nothing else they could do.

"Man, would I like to punch that big blowhard right in the mouth!" Joe said through gritted teeth when they were seated in their yellow sports sedan.

"Don't let him get under your skin," Frank advised, though he, too, was seething. "Maybe once we crack this case, he'll be talking out of the other side of his mouth!"

The two decided to try the realtor, Jonas Milgrim, next. But once again they found themselves frustrated. "Mr. Milgrim is not in," his secretary announced haughtily.

Joe started to say something but felt Frank's foot nudge his ankle. "When will he be back?" the older Hardy boy inquired.

"I really couldn't say. He's very busy just now and isn't making any appointments."

The young sleuths walked back to their car, which was parked in full view of the glass-fronted real estate office.

"Did you see that guy duck out of sight into his private den just as we walked in?" Joe asked. "I'm sure that was Milgrim."

"Yes, I saw him. He probably recognized us and decided it might be smarter not to talk to us—which probably means he's got something to hide." Frank added with a dry grin, "I think we'll have to see Mr. Jonas Milgrim *without* an appointment."

He drove off, then circled back and parked a block away, in a spot that commanded a clear view of the real estate agency but where they themselves were not likely to be noticed by Milgrim or his secretary.

The afternoon was drawing to a close. The Hardys waited patiently for almost an hour. Soon after five o'clock they saw Milgrim leave. He was a scrawny man with thinning, carroty-orange hair. Quickly he got into his car in a small parking lot next to the office building and drove away.

Frank followed the silver-gray station wagon, which was headed east. As they drove, the business and store frontage gradually gave way to a more residential area. Milgrim was going faster and faster. Presently he turned off into a slanting side street that led to the Shore Road.

"He's spotted us!" Frank muttered between his teeth.

The words were barely out of his mouth when the silver station wagon shot ahead at high speed!

8   *The Black Shadow*

Scarcely pausing for a stop sign, Milgrim's car shot into the Shore Road. A recently completed expressway now carried much of the rush-hour traffic, so there were few vehicles ahead to slow him down. The realtor threaded his way around them at reckless speed, his foot apparently flooring the gas pedal.

"Wow! Looks like this dingdong *really* doesn't want to talk to us!" Joe gasped tensely.

The Hardys' sports sedan packed more than enough power to keep the wagon in sight, but Frank had no wish to provoke an accident.

"Maybe I'd better let the guy go," he said uneasily.

A moment later the decision was taken out of his hands as the silver station wagon swung left without the slightest attempt to brake!

Careening on two wheels, it cut through an opening in the Shore Road's divider island, ignored a traffic signal and headed up a tree-shaded hillside road that led away from the water.

Presumably Milgrim had been hoping his pursuer would be unable to turn in time. But Frank's reflexes responded with the nerveless ease of an expert race driver. He swerved deftly into the left lane, rounded the island and, after waiting only seconds for the divider light to change to green, zoomed up the side road in hot pursuit.

Now that they were off the Shore Road, Frank was less fearful of an accident. "Milgrim just lost any chance of shaking us," he murmured to Joe with a grin. "From here on we're going to stay right on his tail till he pulls over!"

There was no doubt that the yellow sports sedan was faster, nimbler and better designed for a rough uphill chase than the wagon. But Frank was saved the trouble of proving this when the winding, poorly paved side road brought the race to a sudden, violent conclusion.

The softly sprung wagon was already bouncing and jouncing as it sped along when a pothole and a sharp bend in the road threw it totally out of control. Milgrim tried frantically to straighten out, but his car fishtailed and slid wildly off the road. It ended up on the rough shoulder, tilted at a perilous angle, with one rear wheel hanging over a ditch.

Frank braked smoothly to a stop, and the Hardys jumped out. The station wagon's engine was roaring, and one rear wheel was churning while its driver struggled to get back on the road. At last Milgrim gave up and stared out the car window as the two young sleuths came up to talk to him.

"Need any help?" Frank inquired mildly.

"Stay away from me!" the scrawny realtor snarled. "I have nothing to say to you!" He was shaking all over with an evident mixture of anger and fright.

"We haven't asked you anything yet," Joe pointed out. "So how come you're scared of us? Is there some reason you can't talk about the Blackwing Mansion?"

Milgrim's tawny eyes flickered in fear, as if

the Hardys had just threatened him with a knife. "I told you to keep away from me!" he said, his voice quavering. "Now leave me alone or I'll call the police!"

Joe was about to flare back at him, but Frank put a hand on his brother's arm, realizing there was no hope of reasoning with the realtor in his present upset state. "You'd better call *some-one*," he advised Milgrim, "or you'll be stuck here in this ditch all night. Come to think of it, we'll call for a tow truck over our CB radio—there may not be a phone in reach."

Milgrim's only response was a wild-eyed, open-mouthed stare.

After radioing for help, the Hardys drove away. Joe said, "That creep knows something, all right! But what's he so worried about?"

Frank shrugged. "He was too scared to talk, that's for sure."

Aunt Gertrude was reading the newspaper when the boys arrived home.

"Did you talk to Madame Xavia?" Frank asked her.

"Indeed I did!" she replied in her usual peppery fashion. "If you ask me, that woman's a possible mental case—or if not, there's more to this mystery than you boys bargained for!"

"What exactly did she say, Aunty?" Joe inquired.

"At first she wouldn't talk—either about that letter she sent the Allens or the Blackwing Mansion itself—just kept throwing out a smoke screen about how she wasn't free to discuss the matter. Well, I soon put a stop to that nonsense! I let her know in no uncertain terms that I intended to get to the bottom of this affair."

"So then what happened?" Frank pursued.

"She finally broke down and gabbled about the terrible psychic vibrations she was getting. She claims she's heard mysterious voices at night, prophesying doom to the residents of the Blackwing Mansion, and says she's even glimpsed a black-winged figure soaring in the moonlight outside her bedroom window!"

The Hardy boys stared at each other in astonishment. "What do you make of all that, Aunt Gertrude?" Joe asked.

"Hmph. All I'm sure of at this point is that Madame Xavia is certainly convinced the mansion's haunted. Beyond that . . . well, this Blackwing mystery may be even more tangled than we suspect. I've a feeling you two will have your hands full solving it."

"We already do," Frank confessed wryly. Then he and Joe reported their own adventures of that afternoon.

"Which reminds me!" Aunt Gertrude snapped her bony fingers. "I just remembered where I read about the Blackwing Mansion."

"Where?" Frank asked excitedly.

"In the Bayport *News*. They ran a series of articles telling all about the history of the Blackwing Mansion."

"Hey, we ought to read those!" Joe exclaimed to his brother.

Frank nodded. "Right. It'll be interesting to find out if anyone else ever saw that flying black ghost before the Allens moved in."

After dinner the two boys drove to the public library. They knew that the library kept copies of the local newspaper for several years back. The paper itself provided a yearly index of its news stories and features, so the Hardys had no difficulty finding the exact dates of the articles in question.

A librarian brought out the newspapers, and the boys took them to a table in a quiet alcove to pore over them.

Somewhat to their surprise, they learned that the series of feature stories had been prompted by the fact that Mr. and Mrs. Allen had purchased the famous old landmark and begun restoring it to its former picturesque splendor.

They also learned that the old slaver Moray Thaw—or Captain Blackwing, as he was known—was not its original builder. Ironically, the house had first belonged to abolitionists, who opposed slavery and were determined to do away with it. The mansion, in fact, had been a station on the "Underground Railway," the escape route by which runaway slaves were smuggled out of the country and over the Canadian border to freedom. Captain Thaw, it seemed, had shown great glee in buying up the mortgage and foreclosing on the house's original owners after they had spent their family fortune and gone into debt carrying out the fight against slavery.

"Tough luck," Joe murmured, "but at least they won their fight in the end."

"And that old blackbirder sure didn't wind up having the last laugh," added Frank, who was reading ahead of his brother. He pointed to a column in the final article of the series and slid the paper over to Joe.

The passage told how Captain Thaw had later been found dead, sprawled on the floor of the house, with his face contorted in a spasm of terror. One popular story among the neighbors was that his soul had been carried off by the devil. Thereafter, the house was said to be haunted, but the article spoke only vaguely of noises heard at night and made no mention of the flying Blackwing ghost.

"Whew!" Joe said in a low voice as he finished reading the passage. "If I were the Allens, I'm not sure I would've *wanted* to buy that place!"

Late that night, when the Hardy household was asleep, the two brothers were awakened by the ringing of the telephone. Both jerked upright from their pillows with the same thought in mind.

"That could be Dad!" Joe exclaimed.

"I know! Let's get it quick before Mom or Aunt Gertrude answers!" Frank was already flinging off the covers and leaping to his feet.

As the boys were about to dart toward the doorway leading out into the hall, Joe grabbed his brother's arm and pointed. "Frank, *look!*"

In the moonlit semidarkness a black-winged figure could be seen silhouetted against the bedroom wall!

9 Butterfly Bait

Frank gasped in astonishment as he stared at the sinister shadow. He turned toward the window to see what was causing it.

A strange, black-winged object was pressed against the screen!

Both boys darted to examine it. But before they reached the window, the thing flitted off into the darkness!

"Where'd it go?" Joe exclaimed in angry frustration, trying to peer through the screen.

"Good question!" Frank said grimly. "For that matter, where'd it come from?" Then he gave up with a shrug. "I'd better go see who's on the phone."

The words were barely out of his mouth when the telephone stopped ringing.

"Rats!" Joe muttered.

To make the situation even more vexing, the phone had jangled just long enough to awaken both their mother and Aunt Gertrude.

"Probably a wrong number," Frank told the two women as they opened their bedroom doors and looked out into the hallway with anxious, inquiring expressions.

He spoke in a soothing voice so as not to alarm them, and made no mention of the weird black shadow. Later, when he and Joe were sure their mother and aunt had gone back to sleep, they dressed hastily and hurried outside to search for signs of an intruder. But the search proved fruit-less.

Next morning after breakfast, however, Frank decided to check again in broad daylight. "What are you looking for?" Joe asked. "Anything specific?"

"No, just thought I might spot something we'd missed last ni—" Frank broke off abruptly, his eyes narrowing with sudden interest. "Hey, get a load of this, Joe!"

He pointed to a scrape mark on the heavy drainpipe that ran up one corner of the house near their bedroom window.

Joe whistled softly. "Looks fresh, all right! Think that could've been made last night?"

"Why not?" Frank rubbed his jaw, his face taking on a thoughtful frown. "Try this for size. Suppose someone makes a cardboard cutout of that blackwing figure, shinnies up our drainpipe and sticks it on our bedroom screen, with a string dangling down. Then he has a confederate dial our number—"

"So the phone ringing will wake us up," Joe cut in eagerly. "The intruder's hiding under our window, and when he hears our voices and we come rushing to see what's out there, he simply jerks the string and the blackwing ghost disappears!"

"Exactly—the idea being to scare us out of our wits and convince us the Allens really *are* being haunted by some evil spirit."

"Neat trick," Joe commented dryly, "but if he's aiming to scare us off the case, he's wasting his time!"

The Hardys decided to enlist the help of their father's top operative, Sam Radley. After driving to his apartment, which also served as his office, they told Radley about their midnight meeting with their dad on Barmet Bay. They also filled him in on the Allen case.

Joe went on. "What can you tell us about this guy Clyde Peachum, Sam—anything?"

Radley knit his brow. "Not much. He's what they call a sharpshooter—a money man who's ready to cut any kind of deal where he sniffs a chance for a quick profit."

"What kind of deals?"

"Oh, mainly building and real estate development. But that's not all. The guy's a slick operator with lots of political pull. From what I hear, he'll put up capital for almost any sort of undertaking so long as there's likely to be a big payoff in it for Clyde Peachum."

"Any idea why he might be interested in the Blackwing Mansion?" Joe pursued.

Sam Radley shook his head. "No, but I'll check it out and let you know if I turn up any leads."

Frank had been mulling over another idea. "Look," he mused aloud, "whoever lost that butterfly necklace may not realize it got snagged on a tree branch."

"Maybe not," Joe agreed. "So what?"

"For all he knows, the clasp may have come

loose of its own accord and the ornament just dropped in the street somewhere. So why don't we put a lost-and-found ad in the paper and see if anyone answers it?"

Joe's eyes kindled with interest. "Hey, that's not a bad idea!"

Radley nodded. "But take my advice and don't put your own phone number in the ad. Remember, whoever's behind this business may be dangerous. He may get nasty if he suspects the Hardy boys are trying to bait a trap for him."

"What would you suggest, Sam?"

"Use a telephone answering service as a blind. Here's one I've used myself." He jotted down the name and phone number of the answering service on a slip of paper and handed it to Frank. "I'll arrange it, if you like."

"Great! Do that, please."

The Hardys quickly composed an ad saying that a butterfly necklace had been found in Bayport; to reclaim it, the owner should call the number Sam Radley had jotted down. Then they drove to the business office of the Bayport *News*.

"Can you run this today?" Frank asked the young woman behind the desk.

"Sure," she replied. "Since you're turning in

the ad before eleven, it'll appear in the afternoon edition of the *News*."

The Hardys drove home. Shortly after they arrived, they received a call from one of their friends, Phil Cohen. "You guys coming out to the airfield today?" he inquired.

"Sure," said Joe, who had answered the phone. "Who else is going?"

"Well, Tony can't make it. He's still working on that construction job for his dad. But Biff Hooper and I will be there. You realize if we all get cooking on this, we could have our ultralight airborne by next week!"

Joe was thrilled at the prospect. "Right on, Phil! You can count on us!"

Ultralight airplanes, which at first were little more than hang gliders with small engines attached, had become one of the most popular means of sport flying. Since the craft were easy and relatively cheap to build and operate, the Hardys and their friends had begun working on a homemade ultralight of their own. Pilot Jack Wayne, owner-operator of the Ace Air Service, whose planes were often chartered for special flights by Fenton Hardy, gave the boys help and advice on their project.

Other ultralight enthusiasts were present

when Frank and Joe arrived at the airfield that afternoon. Most were tinkering with their own craft. One ultralight plane was already aloft, soaring and swooping gracefully during a lull in the airport's commercial traffic.

The Hardys quickly changed into grease-stained coveralls in the hangar, then joined their friends, who were covering one of the wings with glistening plastic film. Frank and Joe pitched in to help draw the skin taut over the aluminum-tubing framework.

The young sleuths brought Biff and Phil up to date on the latest developments in the Black-wing mystery. Intrigued by what they overheard of the weird case, other sport fliers gathered around to listen. Joe noticed one of them, named Creech, giving him and his brother nasty looks and wondered why.

"You think some weirdo's flying over that old mansion in a black ultralight?" an onlooker queried.

Frank shrugged. "Who knows? If that's the answer, it must be different from any ultralight I've ever heard of. This one flits around *silently*."

Joe added with a half-joking grin, "Any of you guys ever hear of a black flying contraption that makes no noise?"

Nobody had. "That's like asking if anyone's ever heard of a silent power lawn mower," cracked a mechanic known as Sarge. "Tell you what it does remind me of, though—a fighter pilot I used to know in the Air Force."

"How so?"

"Oh, he always had a black-winged insignia painted on the side of his plane—called it the *Black Butterfly*. That was his nickname, too. And every so often on landings, he liked to cut power and glide in silently, just to show what a hotshot jet jockey he was. In fact, come to think of it, I believe he'd trained as a glider pilot."

Joe's grin had given way to a look of interest. "What happened to him?"

"Search me. I heard he left the Air Force and flew in Africa as a mercenary fighter pilot, but I don't know if that's true or just scuttlebutt."

"What was his name?" Joe asked curiously.

Sarge shrugged. "I don't remember. It's been a long time." Joe pulled his brother aside. "Interesting, huh?" he remarked.

"Sure," Frank replied thoughtfully. "That mention of the word *butterfly* and then Africa may be just a coincidence, but it made me think of that necklace you found in the tree."

"Me, too. Frank, Jack Wayne served in the Air Force. Why don't I ask him if he ever heard of the Black Butterfly?"

"Good idea."

Joe started off across the airfield toward the office of the Ace Air Service. Jack Wayne—lean, rangy and brown-haired—was seated behind the counter. He listened to Joe's question, then frowned as he searched his memory. "The Black Butterfly? . . . Hmm, it doesn't ring any bells offhand, but I'll ask around and see if any of the pilots I know have ever heard of him."

"We'll appreciate it, Jack. Thanks a lot." Joe headed back to the hangar apron, where his brother, Phil and Biff were working on their homemade ultralight.

As he passed the open door of the hangar, Joe's curiosity was aroused by someone he glimpsed inside. A skulking figure had just darted behind a stack of crated engine parts, as if to avoid being noticed.

Joe turned abruptly and strode into the hangar. He was suspicious not only because of the furtive way the man had ducked out of sight but also because the Hardys and their friends had rented lockers and workbench space in the hangar for their project.

His suspicions were sharpened when he recognized the lurking figure as Matt Creech, the fellow who had been scowling at him and Frank.

"What're you doing here, Creech?" Joe demanded.

"Looking for a tool, if it's any of your business."

"My friends and I rent this workspace," Joe retorted. "What kind of tool did you want?"

"A . . . a drill gauge," Creech faltered. His face turned sullen. "But if you're all that worried about lending anything out, forget it!"

He tried to brush past Joe, who said, "If you want to borrow something, ask for it. I just don't like sneaks."

Creech's voice turned ugly. "Who are you calling a sneak?"

"If the shoe fits, wear it," Joe snapped.

"Listen, you wise-mouth little punk—!" Creech reached out to grab the front of Joe's coveralls, but the Hardy boy slapped his adversary's hand away and cocked his fist for action, in case Creech cared to push matters to a fight.

They might have come to blows, had Frank not appeared at the hangar just then looking for his brother.

"Hey, Joe!" he called. "Let's get over to the parking lot pronto! Chet just pulled in and says there's a message coming over our car radio!"

10 Nocturnal Swoop

Frank stopped short as he noticed Joe's doubled-up fist and the belligerent way he and Matt were confronting each other. "Anything wrong?" he inquired in an even voice.

"Nothing important," Joe said scornfully. His eyes challenged Creech to put up or shut up.

There was a moment of tense silence. Then Creech turned away with a vengeful glare and left the hangar. Joe relaxed and walked off with his brother, heading for the airfield parking lot.

"What was that all about?" Frank asked.

"I caught him snooping around our part of the hangar and called him on it. For some reason he was also putting the evil eye on us just before I went to see Jack Wayne."

"So I noticed. What's his problem?"

"Don't ask me—but maybe we'd better watch that guy from now on. He may be nursing a grudge."

Frank nodded thoughtfully. "Good idea. What did you find out from Jack?"

"He's never heard of the *Black Butterfly*, but he'll ask around among his pilot friends."

Chet Morton's jalopy was pulled up alongside the Hardy's yellow sports sedan, which no doubt explained how he had become aware of their incoming call. A red signal light was flashing on their dashboard, and a buzz could be heard from their CB transceiver.

Frank opened the car door, flicked a switch and picked up the hand mike. "H-1 here! Come in, please!"

Sam Radley identified himself over the air and went on. "I just had a call from that phone-answering service. There's already been one response to your newspaper ad."

"Hey, fast work!" Frank exclaimed. "Who was the caller?"

"He didn't give any name. Jane Duffy, who took the call, didn't want to let on that the

93

number was an answering service, in case that might make the guy suspicious. So she stalled and said the person who found the necklace was out but would return in about an hour. He told her he'd call back."

"Great! We'll get right over there, Sam. Where's Jane's office located?"

"Ewell Building, on the corner of Main and Hudson, second floor. I'll meet you there in case anything develops."

"Thanks a lot, Sam!"

The Hardy boys changed out of their coveralls, then drove to the business district of Bayport and found a parking space near the Ewell Building. Sam Radley had already arrived at the tiny office of the telephone-answering service.

"Nothing yet," he reported as they walked in. "But it may not be too long, if the guy keeps his word about calling back."

While the three waited, Sam told the Hardys what he had learned about Clyde Peachum. "He's trying to put together a big-enough parcel of land to erect a high-rise condominium. According to a banker who's a friend of mine, Peachum's already invested half a million bucks in buying up property for the project—but to complete it, he needs the grounds of the Black-wing Mansion. If the Allens won't sell, the condominium may never get built, and all that money may go down the drain."

"Wow!" Joe gasped. "No wonder he's so anxious to get the Allens out of their house."

"Peachum's a high-powered wheeler-dealer," Sam said dryly. "One way or another he usually gets whatever he's after."

"In that case, maybe he's already got that realtor, Jonas Milgrim, under his thumb," Frank conjectured shrewdly. "He could have had Milgrim act as a front man, trying to buy back the property. Then, when that didn't work, Peachum himself got into the act and tried to pressure the Allens still more."

"Sure, that figures," Sam Radley agreed. "I'll keep nosing around and let you know if I find out anything more."

The Hardys thanked him. "By the way, Sam," Joe added, "suppose this guy who answered the ad calls back and he sounds like the real owner of the necklace. Where should we meet him?"

"Not at our house," Frank voted. "If he's mixed up in the Blackwing caper and discovers the ad was placed by us, it would scare him off!"

"You're right," Sam agreed. "Tell you what.

Several other detectives and I have an apartment we often use as a cover address in our work. It's in a tenement house on Fremont Street, near the docks—we rent it by the month. You could meet him there."

Sam jotted the address on a slip of paper he tore from his pocket notepad. Just as he was handing it to the Hardys, the woman who ran the answering service—Jane Duffy—turned from her switchboard and signaled frantically.

"Here's your caller!"

Frank picked up an extension phone. "Hello?"

"I'm calling back about that ad you put in the paper, about a butterfly necklace."

"That's right." Frank found it hard to judge from the voice what sort of person the caller was. Aloud he said, "Are you the owner of the necklace?"

"I sure am."

"Where exactly did you lose it?"

"Probably somewhere on Indian Road—at least that's where I was when I noticed it was gone."

"That's where I found it, all right." Frank tried to sound very matter-of-fact and convincing. "What does this necklace you lost look like?"

"It's got a silver chain, and the ornament attached to it is also made of silver. It's shaped like a butterfly, about two or three inches wide, and the wings are enameled in blue and gold."

"That checks," Frank said, "so it must be yours. What's your name, by the way?"

The caller hesitated. "Er, Bill Johnson."

"Well, you can pick up the necklace any time, Mr. Johnson. But you'd better let me know when you're coming, so I can make sure to be in."

Another brief hesitation. "What about nine o'clock this evening?"

"Okay, fine," said Frank.

"Er, what's your name and address?"

Frank grinned at his brother and Sam Radley as he replied, "Franklin—Joe Franklin." Then he read off the address on Fremont Street that Sam had jotted down, adding, "I live in Apartment 312 on the third floor."

"Right, I've got it. Incidentally, you have a twenty-five-dollar reward coming, and I'll also pay you back for the cost of the ad, okay?"

"Fine! See you tonight at nine then, Mr. Johnson." Frank hung up the phone and circled his thumb and forefinger at Joe and Sam. "That's our man, all right!"

The boys ate dinner at home, then fidgeted impatiently till dusk settled over Bayport.

Shortly after eight they drove to Fremont Street. Sam Radley was waiting for them outside. He had already inserted a grimy card, lettered with the name *Franklin,* above the bell button for 312 in the building's vestibule.

There was no elevator. As they trudged up to the third floor, Radley said, "We can't be sure this creep won't come armed, so I think it may be smarter to stake out the setup from across the street. There's a vacant lot over there, with enough bushes and litter to give us cover."

"How'll we know when Johnson comes?" Joe asked.

"No problem. I've got a radio transmitter rigged in the apartment that'll beep us when anyone rings the bell." Radley pulled out a small walkie-talkie to show the Hardys. "As soon as we hear the signal, we'll run across the street and corner him in the building. I figure the three of us can subdue him."

After double-checking the transmitter hookup inside the place, the three retired to the vacant lot across the street from the tenement. By now, complete darkness had fallen. However, a streetlight illuminated the building entrance.

Sam and the Hardys found empty boxes to sit on and made themselves comfortable, screened by underbrush and shrubbery from the view of passersby. The moon was clouded over, and the tenement—a long, low, three-story structure—loomed dimly against the misty night sky.

Minutes dragged by. Then Joe cried, "Hey, look!" as the others gaped in surprise.

Something huge and black-winged had just swooped down on the flat roof of the tenement house!

11 Smoke Screen

For a moment the three watchers were too astounded to react. Frank found his voice first, as the black-winged object glided to a stop near the end of the roof. "It must be some kind of aircraft!"

"Flown by the guy we're staked out to catch!" Joe added.

There was not enough moonlight to discern exactly what was happening on the rooftop across the street; but a smaller moving shadow seemed to detach itself from the dark craft that had just winged down from the night sky.

"There he goes!" Sam Radley exclaimed,

springing up from their hiding place. "Come on! He can get down into the building on one of the fire escapes!"

All three raced across the street, the Hardys close at Sam's heels. He burst into the tenement vestibule, keyed open the inside front door and led the way upstairs two steps at a time.

"With luck we can still corner him in the apartment while he's searching for the necklace!" Radley said over his shoulder as they dashed upward.

After they reached the third floor, the three ran through the worn-carpeted hallway to apartment 312. Radley stuck his key in the lock and turned it.

Just as he pushed the door open, there was a startling explosion as if a firecracker had gone off inside. The next moment a cloud of greenish-gray smoke billowed into the hall!

"He's set off a gas grenade!" Frank cried.

Sam Radley was coughing and groping blindly for the wall switch. But even when his fingers found it and a dull glow illuminated the room, he had difficulty seeing farther than a foot in front of him.

"A smoke screen for our friend's getaway!" Joe choked out the words. His eyes were smarting from the acrid fumes, and even the shallow breaths he drew were irritating his throat and nasal passages.

"Use a handkerchief!" Frank advised. Holding one over his nose and mouth, he tried to orient himself by what Sam had told him about the apartment's layout. "Window's on the left, isn't it, Sam?"

"Check! And wide open, too, probably. Something tells me our bird's already flown the coop!"

Frank, Joe and Sam bumped into one another while they groped their way to the window. The air in the room was clearing as the gray-green vapor drifted outside, and it quickly became obvious that Sam's guess was correct—the intruder was gone!

"Is there a fire escape in reach?" Frank asked Sam Radley, who was craning out the window.

"Yes, it connects to the apartment next door, but it's easy to swing over." He clambered out on the sill, hooked a leg onto the fire escape and soon managed to pull himself from the window ledge onto the narrow stairs. Frank and Joe followed.

Although the fire escape itself went no higher than the third floor, a separate metal ladder ran from there to the top of the roof parapet. Sam and the Hardys scampered up, one at a time.

Too late. By the time they reached the roof, the mysterious black-winged aircraft was silently soaring aloft and soon disappeared into the cloudy darkness.

"Of all the rotten luck!" Joe burst out angrily.

"I wonder what clued him in that we were setting a trap?" Frank said, straining his eyes skyward.

"Nothing," Radley guessed. "He probably just decided to take no chances."

"But how did he know which window to climb into?" said Joe.

"I suppose he came here and checked out the setup soon after Frank gave him the address over the phone," Radley replied.

Frank was inclined to agree. "He could have waited in his car till he saw someone go in who looked like a tenant—maybe with an armload of groceries—and then followed the person inside before the vestibule door slammed. Or maybe he just rang several doorbells on the chance someone would buzz him in. Then all he'd have to do would be to see where apartment 312 was located."

Presumably, had a light been on in the window of 312, indicating that someone was there, the intruder would either have waited on the fire escape till the coast was clear or taken off immediately.

Both Hardys were furious at the failure of their plan to catch the person who was terrorizing the Allens. But at least they now had definite evidence indicating that the winged black phantom was a flying device operated by a human being. Yet neither could guess how it worked.

"Let's ask Jack Wayne," Joe proposed as the two brothers sat talking in their car after saying good night to Sam Radley.

"Sure can't hurt," Frank agreed. "He might come up with a useful lead."

Knowing the Ace Air Service was often open until midnight or later, the Hardys drove to the airport. Sure enough, Jack himself was in the office, seated behind the counter, still busy with paperwork from the day's flights.

"Hi, fellows," he said, looking up from his desk. "What brings you two here at this hour? Don't tell me you're wrestling with another mystery?"

"We are," Frank replied. "And this one could be right up your alley, Jack. It's an aeronautical mystery."

The Hardys described the weird black craft they had just observed. After listening to their story, however, Jack Wayne was as baffled as they were. "How long is the roof of this tenement house?" he inquired.

Joe hesitated. "Oh, about fifty or sixty feet, wouldn't you say, Frank?"

"No more than that," his brother agreed.

Jack shook his head dubiously. "That's a pretty short runway, even for an ultralight. And you say the thing flies *silently*?"

When the boys nodded, he went on with a frown. "That makes any kind of answer even harder to come up with. It takes power to fly, and an internal-combustion engine makes noise . . . unless of course the joker's flying on some kind of battery-powered electric motor. But that explanation's as farfetched as a silent engine."

"How about a *muffled* engine?" put in Frank.

The pilot shrugged. "With a good muffler, you can tune an engine down to a gentle purr, but even so it makes *some* noise. You'd be bound to hear him, especially on takeoff—unless he has a radically advanced muffler that's superior to anything that's been developed so far—at least anything *I've* heard of."

Jack Wayne stuffed a sheaf of papers into an

envelope and clipped the flap shut. "By the way," he added, "I've got a bit of news for you two."

"Hope it's good," said Joe with a wry grin. "Let's hear it."

"It's about that fighter pilot called the Black Butterfly. A guy who knew him touched down here this evening on his way to Montreal—in fact, they were squadron mates in the Air Force."

"Was he able to give you any information?" Frank inquired eagerly.

"Some," Jack replied. "Part of it you already know. The Black Butterfly's name was Max Kirby, and as you said, after he got out of the Air Force, he flew in Africa as a mercenary. Then he returned to the USA and retired to civilian life . . . but he's now dead."

"Dead?" Joe echoed quizzically.

"That's right. According to the pilot I talked to, Kirby died in an accident a year or two ago."

The Hardys stood, letdown expressions on their faces. Although they had no evidence connecting him to the Blackwing mystery, the Black Butterfly had somehow seemed a promising lead—until now.

"Thanks for the info, Jack," Frank said, and

added wryly, "So much for *that* theory!"

Next morning at breakfast the boys talked over the case. "If you come right down to it," Frank mused, "that butterfly necklace is the one solid clue we have."

"Maybe so," Joe said gloomily. "But what does it tell us?"

"Well, it doesn't tell us who's pulling this Blackwing caper. But we do know two things that may be important."

"What two things?"

"One, this ornament on the necklace isn't just an *imaginary* butterfly—it's copied from a real species—*Prepona deiphile*, Mr. Drexel called it. That sounds to me as though our ghost may be a butterfly expert, or at least a butterfly fancier."

Joe nodded as he spread some strawberry jam on a piece of toast. "Sounds reasonable. What's the other thing?"

"Drexel said this butterfly was a South American species, from Brazil," Frank replied. "Yet the ornament itself was made in a North African Moorish country like Morocco. So the Moorish craftsman who made it wasn't likely to know what a *Prepona deiphile* looked like out of his own head."

107

"In other words, you're saying somebody *ordered* the silver ornament from him—somebody who showed him what the butterfly's wings should look like."

"Right. Maybe a South American, or a traveler who'd *been* to South America."

"Not necessarily," Joe argued. "He might just be a butterfly buff who knew what a *Prepona deiphile* looked like."

Frank nodded thoughtfully. "True. But in either case, why would he want an ornament made up to resemble that particular species?"

Joe wiped some jam off his mouth and said, "Search me, but it might not hurt to find out all we can about that butterfly. Who knows? We might even turn up a fresh clue that way."

"Maybe you've got something there. Why don't I call Drexel and see if he can tell us where to get more information." Frank rose from the table and went to the hallway phone, where he dialed the wealthy collector's number.

When he hung up a little later, he turned to Joe, who had followed him out of the dining room. "We're in luck! Drexel says the *American Geographic* magazine featured an article on *Prepona* butterflies just over a year ago."

"Great. Let's go look it up right now."

The Hardys drove to the public library, where

Frank asked for a copy of the magazine. He and Joe took it to a table and pored over the article avidly. Although they found it interesting, they were disappointed when neither could glean any useful new facts from it.

Just as Frank was about to close the magazine, Joe hissed, "Hey, wait a second!"

"Why? Did we miss something?"

"Take a look at that picture of a *Prepona*."

Frank wrinkled his brow. "What should I look for?"

"Forget the pretty colors. Just notice the general wing shape."

There was a brief silence. Then Frank gasped. "Jumpin' Jupiter! That looks like the shadow we saw on our bedroom wall the other night!"

"Right. And also the shape of the Blackwing ghost!"

12 Café Clue

The Hardys digested this latest clue.

"I'm not sure how much this helps us," Frank murmured, "but at least it proves one thing: Whoever lost that necklace in the tree must be the joker who's flying the Blackwing Ghost."

Joe nodded thoughtfully, remembering the previous night's carefully baited trap, which had come so close to snaring the culprit. "No wonder our friend was so anxious to get the necklace back," he said.

"Guess we didn't waste our time here after all." Frank idly flipped through the pages of the magazine before returning it to the reference librarian. "Hey, get a load of this, Joe!" he suddenly added.

"What's that?"

"An article on the old slave ship captains."

Joe's eyes lit up. "Does it mention Captain Blackwing?"

"Dunno—the article's pretty long. Looks interesting, though, whether it mentions him or not. I think I'll take it home."

Frank checked out the magazine at the library counter. Then the two boys headed back to their car. They had already decided to check the security of their boathouse, in light of the deadly booby trap Frank had discovered following the midnight rendezvous with their father on Barmet Bay. On their way to the waterfront, they stopped at a locksmith's shop to buy a new and more burglarproof door lock, which Frank had read about in one of Fenton Hardy's professional police journals.

On reaching the harbor, they parked near their boathouse. Before installing the new lock, they carefully inspected the old one. Frank pointed to several tiny scratch marks near the keyhole. Though faint, they were clearly visible in broad daylight. "It's been jimmied, all right," he commented. "That's how the creep who planted the Molotov cocktail got in."

"How do we know he hasn't been back since then?" Joe asked.

"Don't worry." With his fingernails Frank plucked a long paintbrush bristle out of the door crack. "I stuck that in place as a telltale after I disarmed the firebomb. If he'd come back, the bristle would have fallen out when he opened the door."

Joe grinned. "Smart thinking, Frank! That's why I always like to have you along when I tackle a mystery case."

The Hardy boys quickly installed the new lock, then started back to their car. On the boardwalk Joe noticed two men standing in front of a nearby café. They had been talking earnestly, but as the Hardys went past, they suddenly hurried inside.

"Whoa! Hold it a sec," Joe muttered to Frank.

"How come?"

"Did you see those two guys who just ducked into the café?"

"No. What about them?"

"One was Matt Creech, that blowhard I had a run-in with at the airfield. For some reason he seemed awfully anxious not to be seen!"

Frank's eyes narrowed. "Just like in the hangar, huh?"

"Right! Let's find out what he's up to!"

The two boys rushed back to the café. But when they peered in through the window, Creech and his companion were nowhere in sight!

Joe angrily socked his fist into his open palm. "Must've ducked out the back way! I'd say that *proves* something fishy's going on!"

Frank shrugged philosophically. "Maybe so, but there's not much we can do about it now."

"Don't be too sure of that!"

As soon as they got home, Joe got the Identikit from his father's study and proceeded to make up a composite likeness of Creech's companion by piecing together the right kind of hair, eyes, nose, ears, and so forth.

The portrait was that of a heavy-jowled man with a big nose, thinning hair and a gaunt, deeply lined face.

"If this guy can be identified," Joe told his brother, "it may give us a clue to whatever monkey business Creech is into."

Frank nodded approvingly. "Good work. Are you going to photograph it?"

"Sure, let's make some prints we can hand out."

Soon after lunch the Hardys finished their

photographic chore. When they returned to the house from their detective lab over the garage, the doorbell rang. Frank answered it.

"You're one of the Hardy boys, right?" said the tall, swarthy man who was standing on the porch.

"Yes."

"Thought I'd recognized you. My name's Nagel. I'm a free-lance magazine writer. May I come in and talk to you for a few minutes?"

Frank hesitated. "My brother and I don't usually give interviews, Mr. Nagel."

"This isn't exactly an interview," the stranger replied. "You see, I'm working on a story, and I thought you might be able to help me out with a little information. I won't even mention your names, if you don't want me to."

"Well, okay. But we're rather busy, so we can't talk long, Mr. Nagel."

When he was seated in the living room, the visitor explained that he was writing a series of "profiles" on local realtors for a certain real estate magazine. "This week I'm doing a story on Jonas Milgrim," he went on. "The other day I went to see him, but it was late in the afternoon and he'd already left. In fact, I saw him driving off. Then I noticed you two take off after him,

114

and I thought I recognized you as the Hardy boys from pictures I saw of you in the newspaper after one of your recent cases."

"Mind telling us where all this is leading?" Joe broke in bluntly.

Nagel responded with a shrugging gesture. "Well, not to beat around the bush, I got a definite impression you might have been tailing him. And since you're pretty famous as amateur detectives, I also figured that might mean Milgrim is mixed up in some sort of interesting mystery. Am I right?"

"Could be," Frank parried. "The fact is, Mr. Nagel, whenever we're investigating a case, we try to be as discreet as possible—which means we're not free to talk about it."

Nagel looked annoyed. "At least could you tell me if you suspect him of any wrongdoing?"

"Sorry, we can't."

The visitor continued to ply the Hardy boys with questions but received only guarded responses to each. At last he gave up and left.

As Frank closed the front door behind their departing guest, Joe said, "Did that guy sound phony to you?"

"Let's just say I've got a strong hunch he's no magazine writer."

115

"Same here!"

Before they could discuss the stranger any further, the telephone rang. Joe answered. A hoarse, cracked voice said, "Who'm I talkin' to?"

"Joe Hardy. Who are you?

"Marlinspike McGee."

Joe chuckled as he recognized the caller's name. "Hi, Mr. McGee. What can I do for you?"

Marlinspike McGee was one of the local characters of Bayport. A retired old salt, he lived in a rickety shack on Barmet Beach and supported himself mostly by digging clams and selling bait. "Young feller, I've l'arned somethin' that may interest you and your brother," the old man confided.

"Let's hear it," said Joe.

"Not over the phone! This is too important to take any chances. If you want to come see me, I reckon you know where to find me. *Jest make sure you ain't followed! Understand?*"

There was a loud click as the caller hung up. Startled, Joe related the conversation to his brother and they decided to start out at once.

Driving east toward the Shore Road, Frank glanced in the rearview mirror and muttered, "Don't look now, but a black sedan's tailing us!"

Joe stifled an impulse to glance out the back

window. "Can you make out who's driving it?"

"Not too well. But he sure looks like someone whose picture we've seen."

Joe stiffened in alarm. "What picture?" he queried.

"Remember that guy Dad warned Sam Radley about? We found his mug shot in Dad's files."

"You mean Ranse Hobb?"

"None other," Frank said through gritted teeth. "The strong-arm man employed by that international crook Klaus Kane, whom the CIA and FBI are after!"

13 *Surprise Disguise*

"Do you think you can shake him?" Joe inquired.

"Maybe . . . but let's not try."

The younger Hardy boy looked at his brother curiously. "Why not? We don't want to lead him to someone who may have an important clue to give us, do we?"

"No, but if the man behind us is Ranse Hobb, we don't want him to know we've spotted him, either," Frank replied. "Remember, this guy's a pro, and he could be plenty dangerous. It'll be easier to give him the slip if we pretend we don't even know he's there."

118

Joe grinned. "Good thinking, Sherlock. So what's your plan?"

"Sit tight. You'll see."

Frank turned at the next intersection, taking a main road that led to the Roxford Shopping Mall on the southern outskirts of Bayport. A glance in the mirror showed him the black sedan was still behind them.

Reaching the mall, he drove into a section of the parking lot that adjoined the Ocean View Department Store.

"Still with us?" Joe asked tersely as the two boys got out of their car.

"Yes, but don't look around. He cruised on past us into the next section of the parking lot. I think he's over on the right somewhere."

The boys locked the car, then headed for the store. "Act as if we have shopping to do," Frank told his brother with a grin.

Joe chuckled. "What am I supposed to do?"

"Don't ask stupid questions. Just tell me again about that good-looking blazer you want to buy. Isn't this where you saw it?"

"Hey, come to think of it, that's right." As the young detectives ambled up the aisle of the parking lot, talking and joking, Joe spotted the black sedan out of the corner of his eyes. It matched Frank's expert description perfectly and was parked two rows away, among enough other cars to keep it inconspicuous but in a spot that commanded a clear view of their own yellow sports sedan.

Just as they got inside the store, Frank stopped short and snapped his fingers with an angry mutter.

"What's the matter?" Joe asked.

"I forgot to memorize his license number."

"Want me to go back out and get it?"

"No way! Then he'd *know* we've spotted him. Anyhow, we know what the car looks like and who's driving it."

"You're sure he's Ranse Hobb?"

"Positive. Once we'd both turned in to the mall, he came close enough for me to recognize him."

Joe nodded. "Okay, what now?"

"Find a phone."

Striding through the department store into the concourse of the mall, they soon saw a circular stand of public telephones. Frank tried Biff Hooper's number. Luckily their friend was home.

After hearing about the situation, Biff said, "Be right there. I'll turn into the mall from

Bayside Avenue. You know where the pizza shop is on the ground level?"

"Sure."

"Go there and keep watch out the shop window. That'll give you a clear view of the Bayside entrance. Give me ten minutes."

"Great. And thanks, Biff. We'll owe you one for this."

A quarter of an hour later the Hardys were whizzing away from the mall in Biff's colorfully painted van. All three were laughing.

"How long do you suppose your shadow will camp there?" Biff inquired.

"Who knows?" said Frank. "We'll give him a good long wait."

Presently they pulled off the Shore Road and stopped at the edge of the sand dunes. Biff agreed to stay in the van and keep watch for any suspicious characters who might be lurking in the vicinity. Frank and Joe, meanwhile, set off across the dunes on foot toward Marlinspike McGee's beachfront cottage.

The weatherbeaten shack stood amid a clump of scrub pines, sumac and other straggling shrubbery. Frank knocked on the door. It appeared to have been crudely carpentered out of driftwood that was clean-scrubbed by sand and sea wind. There was a movement of the flour-sack curtain at one of the windows.

Then the door opened, and the old clammer himself peered out at the two boys.

Frank said, "Mr. McGee?"

"Reckon you fellers must be the Hardy boys." The man was clad in a striped seaman's jersey and faded blue jeans held up by red suspenders. His tanned, craggy face was framed by a tangle of grayish-white hair, and a corncob pipe was clenched between his tobacco-stained teeth.

"That's right. He's Frank and I'm Joe," Joe replied.

As they returned his keenly suspicious stare, Joe seemed to detect a twinkle in the old salt's steel-blue eyes.

"C'mon in then, lads. Don't jest stand there like bollards on a dock."

McGee shut the door behind them. Then, as he turned to face the Hardys again, both boys' mouths dropped open in gasps of surprise.

"D-D-Dad!" Frank exclaimed.

Their spare, stoop-shouldered host had suddenly straightened to his full, vigorous height and removed the pipe from his mouth, which was spread in a wide, friendly grin. It was obvious now that he was wearing a wig, but his face was still a strange mixture of Fenton Hardy and Marlinspike McGee. "Things have come to a pretty pass when you young sleuths can't even recognize your own father!"

Dropping his pipe on the table, Mr. Hardy seized his sons by their hands, then swept them into a double bear hug, which they returned enthusiastically.

"It's good to see you, Dad!" Joe said. "We were really worried about you."

"No need to be. Sit down. The chairs are kind of rickety, but they'll hold your weight if you're careful." Mr. Hardy explained that he was renting the shack from the real Marlinspike McGee, who had agreed to take a paid vacation from clamming and beachcombing and go visit his niece in Scituate.

"Whatever happened after we left you on Barmet Bay, Dad?" Frank inquired. "As Joe said, we were really worried—especially after we heard that explosion!"

"Those people tossed a grenade into my boat. But I managed to throw it out before it exploded. It hit a dinghy they were pulling behind their boat."

"Do you have any idea who they were?"

"All I caught was a brief glimpse by the flash

from the explosion, but I'm pretty sure one was Ranse Hobb."

"I just saw him," Frank said.

"Where?" Fenton Hardy was clearly startled.

"In our rearview mirror. He tailed us after we left the house, but we managed to shake him at the Roxford Mall."

"Good work, sons!" Mr. Hardy frowned and rubbed his jaw thoughtfully.

"Any progress on cracking the high-tech plant thefts?" Joe asked.

"Not much, I'm afraid. As of this moment we haven't got any promising leads. All we can do is follow up every single clue—which is mostly a matter of hard, dogged legwork."

The ace manhunter looked keenly interested as the boys filled him in on their own case, the Blackwing mystery. "Hmm. It may be just a coincidence," he remarked, "but on one of those high-tech thefts, a plant guard reported seeing a moving ground shadow."

"Couldn't he see what caused it?" put in Frank.

"Unfortunately, no. When he first saw the shadow, he was in a roofed-over parking area, inspecting several vehicles. Once he got out to look up at the sky, there was nothing there—the shadow had passed out of sight."

"Did he describe the shape of the shadow?"

"Not in his report, anyhow. Apparently he never got that good a look at it."

At Frank's request, Fenton Hardy supplied the boys with a list of the high-technology plant thefts, nine in all, which had occurred during the past year.

As he perused the list, Joe noticed that three of the plants that had been robbed belonged to a firm called Technicom, Inc. "Is it possible the thief may be someone with a special grudge against that company, Dad?" he asked.

Mr. Hardy nodded approvingly. "Good thinking, son. The FBI had the same hunch. However, they checked out that angle, and it never paid off. The likeliest suspect they could come up with was an angry inventor who'd been heard to utter threats against Technicom. Seems he got into a bitter lawsuit with the company and lost."

"Does he have an alibi?"

"Didn't need one. Turns out he died in an accident soon afterward."

Joe showed his father the composite likeness he had made up of the man Matt Creech had been talking to outside the waterfront café. But Mr. Hardy was unable to recognize him from any past criminal case.

"Of course that doesn't prove he's not a law-breaker," the famous detective said. "What about this fellow Creech? Do you have reason to believe he's involved in any racket?"

Joe shrugged. "Not really. But he must be up to something, or else he's nursing a grudge against Frank and me." Joe described Creech's odd behavior at the airfield and the furtive way he had ducked out of sight into the waterfront café.

"You know, I've been thinking about that," Frank spoke up. "Remember a week or so ago, we were talking on the phone at the airport. Mom asked us to stop at the supermarket on our way home and pick up some stuff for Aunt Gertrude."

Joe nodded. "Sure, I remember. Aunt Gertie wanted pie shells ready for baking, for her bridge club luncheon next day."

"Right. Anyhow, I had a pencil in my hand to jot down the brand, and then, while I was standing there at the phone, I happened to see Creech. He had stopped his car just outside the hangar and was fiddling with something in the trunk just as we made eye contact. Creech knows we work with the police sometimes. I wonder if he thinks we were spying on him and reporting to the cops?"

"That might explain his attitude, all right," Joe agreed.

After saying good-bye to their father, who promised to keep as closely in touch as possible, the Hardy boys returned to Biff Hooper's van. At Biff's suggestion, they decided to stop at the airfield and spend the rest of the afternoon working on their ultralight airplane.

When they arrived at the airfield, they found that Chet Morton, Phil Cohen and Tony Prito were already busy on the job. Tony had begun to mount the engine, while the others were assembling the wings. The craft was nearing completion, and by four-thirty the group had it ready for a test flight.

Because of his weight, Chet had understood all along that he would not be the test pilot. The others drew lots to see who would be the first to take the *Silver Falcon* aloft. Joe won.

His pulse beating excitedly, he strapped himself into the open seat of the fragile, shimmering-winged flying machine. His chums fell silent and drew out of the way with other onlookers.

He yanked the starter cord. Then, as the engine putt-putted to life, he gunned the throttle. With a roar, the *Silver Falcon* rolled forward.

Joe's stomach was churning nervously. But as

the ground fell away and the little craft leaped higher and higher into the air in response to the stick, he felt a surge of exhilaration. The wind was stinging his face, and his heart was beating a happy tattoo against his ribs. He waved to his friends below and started to bank for a turn.

Suddenly there was a loud *crack!* and the ultralight lurched wildly. Joe gasped in fear. One of the craft's main struts had broken apart!

14   *Sinister Evidence*

For a brief but terrifying moment Joe almost panicked. The left wing of the tiny ultralight aircraft was flapping scarily, and his seat support began to bounce and shudder under the buffeting of the wind.

As he scanned the situation with a stem-to-stern glance, Joe realized that the *Falcon*'s aluminum-tubing framework had lost its rigidity due to the broken strut. At any moment it might come apart completely in midair, plummeting him to certain death!

With a gulp the boy clenched his jaw and closed his mind to any further thought of disaster. Only cool, clear thinking and steady nerves could save him now. To get down safely, he would have to react fast, keep his wits about him and, as the saying went, fly by the seat of his pants.

Manhandling the stick by sheer muscle power despite the worsening vibrations, Joe straightened out as best he could. Then he eased the stick forward inch by inch. The craft was yawing and wobbling like a kite in the wind— the ground was rushing toward him at terrifying speed!

Joe wanted to close his eyes but couldn't. He was low enough now to glimpse the anxious, horrified expressions on the faces of the onlookers. An instant later came a bone-rattling thump as his wheels hit terra firma!

He must have applied the brakes, since the craft rolled slowly to a halt. But Joe couldn't even remember doing so. All he knew for sure was that Frank and their pals and a horde of spectators were suddenly crowding around him, shouting and cheering.

"You okay, Joe?" Frank asked in a slightly shaky voice.

Joe fumbled with the clasp of his seat belt and staggered to his feet. "I'm sore all over, and my back hurts, but otherwise everything seems to be working."

His words were greeted with a burst of cheers.

"Boy, for a second there I thought you'd have to grow wing feathers to get down in one piece!" Tony Prito wisecracked.

"If you were my size you could have bounced!" Chet added.

Joe responded with another grin to their efforts to ease the tension and cheer him up.

"Never mind all that," Phil Cohen said in a businesslike voice. "Let's find out what went wrong."

"That's pretty obvious," Biff retorted, pointing to the broken strut.

"Sure, the break's obvious—but what made it happen? This design's supposed to be strong enough to carry someone Joe's size with an ample safety margin."

The Hardy boys were already on their knees, inspecting the nature of the break. Both halves of the ruptured tubing were jagged and bent over part of their circumference. But most of the fracture was too sharp and clean to have happened by accident.

"There's your answer," Frank announced grimly. "Someone cut it partway through with a hacksaw."

"And I bet I know who!" Joe said through gritted teeth. He had caught a glimpse of Matt

Creech hovering on the fringe of the circle of onlookers around the wounded *Falcon*. Creech's gaze faltered guiltily as he met the Hardy boy's glance.

All the fear and nervous tension that Joe had repressed while he was airborne came seething to the surface. His temper suddenly boiled over. Before Frank could stop him, he jumped to his feet and elbowed his way through the throng of spectators.

Creech didn't wait to hear or deny the Hardy boy's accusation. He took to his heels and ran!

Joe rushed after him, fighting mad. At this moment only one thing mattered, and that was to land his fist on Creech's jaw as hard as possible. But that pleasure was denied him.

Creech galloped into the parking lot fifty feet ahead of his pursuer. He yanked open his car door, leaped in, gunned the engine and sped off seconds before Joe could get close enough to drag him from behind the wheel.

Frank, Biff and the rest of the group were furious when they reached the scene. "That guy tried to kill Joe and now he's getting away!" Biff ranted. "We must—"

But Frank tried to calm his friends. "He just saved us the trouble of finding out whether he's guilty or not. We'll deal with him later."

Biff Hooper drove the Hardys back to the Roxford Mall. Their yellow sports sedan was still standing where they had left it, but Ranse Hobb's black sedan was nowhere in sight.

After a quick but careful check for any sign of tampering or sabotage, Frank and Joe waved good-bye to Biff and headed home to Elm Street.

"Hmph!" said Gertrude Hardy with a sniff, frowning at the boys severely through her gold-rimmed spectacles as they walked into the dining room. "I trust you two realize you're late for dinner. Your mother and I finally had to start without you."

"Sorry about that, Aunt Gertrude," Frank said contritely, taking his place at the table.

"What kept you?" Laura Hardy asked, but the gentle reproof in her voice was softened by her usual fond smile of greeting.

A quick glance passed between her two sons.

"We, uh, were busy on our ultralight at the airfield, Mom," Frank replied. "Guess we forgot to watch the time."

"We can't eat much, anyhow," Joe added. "Tonight's that beach party at Silver Cove."

"Well, just don't bolt down your food," Miss Hardy warned as her nephews helped themselves to the meat loaf, then passed their plates for potatoes and gravy. "Make sure you chew every bite properly."

"Anything you say, Aunty," Joe mumbled as he hastily forked in a mouthful.

After dinner he and Frank excused themselves to dash upstairs and change into swim trunks and sweat shirts. Then they hurried out to their car in the gathering dusk.

Frank took the wheel. "You know, Joe," he mused as they drove to Callie Shaw's house, "I've a feeling we overlooked something important on that list of high-tech plant thefts Dad gave us."

"Like what?"

Frank frowned and shrugged. "Search me. It's just a hunch, that's all. But something tells me there is a clue staring us right in the face, if we'd just examine the list more carefully."

"Okay, we'll take another look at it tomorrow."

Callie, an attractive, brown-eyed blond girl, was not quite ready when they arrived. But soon she came pattering downstairs in halter and slacks, and the trio took off for the Morton farmhouse to pick up Iola.

By eight o'clock the Hardys and their dates were on their way to Silver Cove. Darkness had fallen, and as they left the outskirts of Bayport behind, the moon came out brightly, gilding the highway and countryside.

It was Callie Shaw who first noticed the weird phenomenon. "What's that black shadow?" she remarked suddenly, pointing ahead. "It seems to be moving right along in front of us."

Frank stiffened to attention, and Joe craned forward from the backseat with a gasp as both recognized the ominous silhouette that had caught her notice.

"Jumpin' Jupiter!" Joe blurted. "That's Blackwing's shadow!"

15 A Startling Deduction

Frank stomped on the brake and brought the car to a screeching halt. He flung open the door and leaped out, followed immediately by Joe.

"There it goes!" Frank cried, pointing skyward.

The flying black phantom was peeling off to the right in a steep spiral climb, and, as they watched, it zoomed away toward the hills bordering the bay. By this time the two girls had gotten out of the car to join the Hardys.

"What on earth *was* that thing?" Iola Morton asked in bewilderment.

"A flying ghost that's been scaring the wits out of a young couple who recently moved into the old Blackwing Mansion," Joe replied. "We think it's actually a manned aircraft—maybe a black ultralight, like the one we've been building with the gang."

"But it made no noise," Callie objected with a puzzled look on her pretty face. "How could an airplane fly so *silently*?"

Frank shrugged, his face grim. "Good question. That's one we can't answer yet."

The teenagers got back in their car and once again took off in the direction of Silver Cove. But a few minutes later Callie cried in alarm, "*It's back!*"

The sinister black shadow was once more skimming the highway just ahead of them!

Again Frank stopped the car, and they leaped out. And again the flying specter soared off into the darkness beyond the hills.

"Looks like our black-winged friend's carrying on a war of nerves," Frank exclaimed in angry frustration.

Joe agreed. "Trying to scare us off the case."

Although the girls were somewhat nervous, the Hardys assured them there was nothing to fear, and the group resumed their ride to the cove. Twice more they sighted the black phantom's shadow flitting along the road within the sweep of their headlights, but Frank and Joe were determined not to give their tormentor the satisfaction of stopping again. In fact, both boys were hoping he might be lured into revealing more details of his spooky aircraft. However, this did not happen. By the time they reached Silver Cove, the ghost had disappeared completely.

A dozen young couples from Bayport High had been invited to the beach party, and most had already arrived. In the excitement of getting the moonlight festivities underway, the Hardys and their dates soon forgot all about Blackwing's shadow.

The surf was still warm from the long day's summer sunshine. The young people stripped down to their swimsuits, and a few started tossing a beach ball back and forth while the others wandered along the sand, gathering driftwood.

Soon cookfires were blazing brightly in the darkness. Most of the couples had brought picnic baskets with hot dogs or hamburger patties for roasting over the flames. But the Hardys and their closest friends were looking forward to a fish fry. Phil Cohen had brought along an inflatable rubber boat. He, Frank and Callie embarked in it with fishlines and bait.

They were hoping a school of fish might be swimming close to the surface at this late hour.

Sure enough, Phil soon hooked a striped bass, and minutes later Frank hauled in a bluegill.

"Hey, what's your secret?" Callie complained to the boys with a wistful grin. "How come I can't—" She broke off with a sudden wide-eyed gasp and pointed upward to her left. *"Look!"*

A sinister dark object was swooping toward them in the moonlight!

"The Blackwing ghost!" Frank cried.

Phil gaped. "So *that's* what it looks like!"

The weird craft was diving lower and lower, growing frighteningly larger as it approached. A glow of light flickered in the sky, and a pang of alarm jolted Frank's pulse.

"Jump out of the boat!" he shouted.

Even before he finished speaking, the black phantom passed directly overhead and a blazing thunderbolt hurtled out of the darkness!

"It's a Molotov cocktail!" Phil gulped and dived into the ocean.

Frank grabbed Callie's hand as they plunged overboard, and all three teenagers struck the water together. The resulting violent splash helped shield them from the bursting flames that followed as the fireball landed in their rubber boat.

Luckily, Frank had insisted they wear life

vests in case they drifted too far from shore. Callie was as good a swimmer as the boys, and with this safety precaution the trio easily stroked their way to the beach.

Their friends greeted them with anxious exclamations and queries as they scrambled out of the water and plodded ashore through the gentle breakers.

"That nut's really after us!" Joe burst out angrily.

"You're telling us," Frank panted as he shook himself off and reached for one of the towels that Iola and Phil's date were offering them. "It was a nasty trick, all right, but now I know one thing for sure."

"What's that?" his brother asked.

"The Blackwing specter has a human pilot, and he wears a tight-fitting black suit. I could see that much, at least, when he leaned out to drop the firebomb."

For a while the vicious attack dimmed the fun of the beach party. But the flying phantom made no further appearance, and the teenagers gradually recovered their high spirits. Once the refreshments had been devoured, couples began dancing on the sand to the music of Biff Hooper's tape player, and as the party drew to a midnight close, all were enjoying themselves thoroughly.

Next morning after breakfast the Hardy boys drove to Sam Radley's place for a meeting. Besides relating the previous night's scary encounter with their black-winged attacker, they also told Radley about the self-styled magazine writer named Nagel who had visited them.

"A tall, swarthy guy?" the detective inquired.

"Right," said Frank. "You know him?"

Sam Radley nodded. "Sure. Nagel's no magazine writer, but he's no crook, either."

"Who is he, then?"

"An investigator for the state realtors' association."

"Wow!" Joe flashed a startled glance at his brother, then turned back to Radley. "How do you know all this, Sam?"

"I found out when I ran a check on Jonas Milgrim. There've been several charges of shady dealings lodged against him with the state licensing board, so the realtors' association decided to investigate him on their own and try to head off a public scandal. And the licensing board's agreed to hold off its own hearing until the results are in."

"Would Milgrim know he's being investigated?" Frank asked.

"Could be. If I found out through the grapevine, it's no big secret. That's probably why Nagel was using the 'magazine writer' line as a cover."

"It may also explain why Milgrim was so afraid to talk to us," Frank pointed out.

Joe pulled the composite he had made up of Matt Creech's mysterious companion out of his pocket and showed it to Sam Radley. "Have you ever seen this guy before?" he asked.

The detective frowned. "Matter of fact, I think I have!"

16 Double Leads

"Who is he?" Joe asked eagerly.

Radley hesitated. "I don't remember his name, but I'd be willing to bet he's a known criminal. I think I've seen his mug on a wanted poster."

"Could he be Klaus Kane?" Frank inquired.

"I just don't know. But I'll check him out right away with the police and the FBI."

Both boys were thoughtful when they drove home. Once they were in the house, Frank took out the list of high-tech plant thefts that Mr. Hardy had given them and studied it closely.

143

"Are you on to something?" Joe inquired.

"Maybe I am. Wait a second!" Frank hurried upstairs to their room and came down a moment later holding the list of butterfly thefts supplied by Bradford Drexel. He compared it with the other list, then looked up triumphantly. "There's a connection, Joe, or I'm a walleyed pike!"

"What sort of connection?"

"See for yourself. The dates dovetail too neatly to be pure coincidence. A few days after each butterfly theft, a high-tech plant burglary took place!"

Joe whistled softly. "You're right! What does it mean, Frank?"

The older boy's face had suddenly taken on a grim expression. "For one thing, it means another plant may be broken into very soon!"

Joe frowned, "How do you figure that?" he asked.

"Simple arithmetic," Frank replied. "As things stand right now, there's been one more butterfly robbery than there have been plant thefts."

"One more butterfly robbery . . . ?" Joe paused uncertainly for a moment, then blurted, "Oh, wait a minute! You're talking about that specimen that was taken from Mr. Drexel's collection?"

"Sure. If that was snatched by the same crooks who stole the other butterflies, then the pattern's not complete yet. Assuming the crimes go in pairs, the Drexel burglary is bound to be followed by another high-tech plant job."

"Wow!" Joe's eyes widened, and he snapped his fingers. "You're right! I think we should tell Dad about this, don't you?"

"Definitely. And the sooner the better. Let's see if we can raise him on the radio!"

The brothers hurried out to their radio setup in the garage lab. They knew their call signal would be picked up loud and clear if their father's transceiver was still located as close to home as Marlinspike McGee's shack on Barmet Beach. And sure enough, there was a quick response on the same frequency.

"FH here. What's up, fellows?"

"We may have stumbled on something that relates to the case you're working on, Dad." Frank reported what Bradford Drexel had told them about the theft of valuable butterflies from collections all over the country, and the odd way in which each such theft seemed to be followed by a high-tech plant robbery. "If I'm right, the

145

gang you're after may pull another job very soon!"

"Hmm . . . that certainly makes sense." Fenton Hardy's voice was grim; he sounded clearly impressed by Frank's theory. "It would also explain why Klaus Kane and his strong-arm stooge, Ranse Hobb, should come to Bayport."

"You mean, because they've got their eye on some plant in the Bayport area?"

"Exactly . . . which would make my presence here especially awkward for them."

"So they tossed that grenade in your boat to get you out of the way before they stage the heist," said Frank, completing his father's unspoken thought.

"It looks that way, son, in light of what you've just told me."

Joe took the microphone. "What's the likeliest high-tech target around here, Dad?"

"Well, there are a number of important defense plants within a ten- to twenty-mile radius of Bayport, as you know. But in terms of new technology that foreign agents would be most eager to get hold of, I'd say Ross Robotics on Highway 19 would be the most tempting firm. Right now that company's turning out the most advanced production robots in the world."

Joe gave a low whistle. "Sounds like just the sort of place where the gang could make a prize haul!"

"No doubt about that," Mr. Hardy agreed. "The company's research-and-development department is probably chock full of top-secret computer data, specs, plans, drawings, what have you—stuff that would be worth a fortune to certain foreign powers."

"How'll you handle this, Dad?" Frank asked.

"The first step is to alert the plant officials and the proper law enforcement agencies. Then we'll see what countermeasures can be taken. As the saying goes, forewarned is forearmed— thanks to this tip you've given me. I'd better contact Ross Robotics right away!"

After finishing their radio conversation with Mr. Hardy, Frank and Joe paced about excitedly. Both felt that this latest clue might not only help crack the case their father was working on but might also shed some new light on their own mystery investigation.

Joe had another thought. "Frank," he mused aloud as he toyed with the silver butterfly necklace, "you pointed out that if this came from Africa, the craftsman who made it wouldn't have known what a *Prepona deiphile* looked like—so

147

it must have been ordered by someone who did know."

"Yes?"

"How about that fighter pilot, Max Kirby? We know he flew in Africa, and if he decorated his plane with a black butterfly, he *may* have been a butterfly fancier or even a butterfly collector."

Frank paused, his eyes lighting with interest. "You're saying that the ornament may have belonged to Kirby?"

"Why not, if he fits the bill."

"No reason at all—in fact, I'd call it a smart hunch, Joe. And another angle just occurred to me that might be worth looking into."

"What's that?"

"Remember how Jack Wayne was told that the *Black Butterfly* pilot died in an accident after he came back to the States? Well, isn't it a bit odd that the same thing happened to that angry inventor Dad told us about—the one who was sore at Technicom. When the FBI checked him out, it turned out he also died in an accident."

"Hey, how about that!" Joe's eyes, too, lit with fresh excitement. "Do you think it's just a coincidence—or is there some connection?"

"I don't know, but let's find out. Maybe Dad can get more information from the FBI."

Frank turned back to the radio, switched it on, and once more beamed out an emergency call signal to Mr. Hardy. This time, however, there was no response, and after a few minutes the boys gave up.

"He may have gone to alert the management at Ross Robotics," Joe conjectured.

Frank nodded. "Probably. In the meantime, let's see if we can find out any more about that pilot Max Kirby."

"From Jack Wayne?"

"Right. If Kirby was once in the U.S. Air Force, he must have a service record. And Jack's a major in the Air Force Reserves. Maybe he can dig up some more information through his Air Force contacts in Washington."

"Good idea!"

The brothers drove to the airport and hurried to the office of the Ace Air Service. Jack Wayne was talking to a customer but broke off as he saw them walk in the door.

"Hi, fellows!" he greeted the boys. "You two showed up at just the right time."

"How come, Jack?"

"Here's someone else who's come up against the same mystery you're working on." Jack Wayne gestured to his customer, a thick-set, broad-shouldered man with iron-gray hair, and made introductions. "Frank and Joe Hardy, this is Mr. Tyler Trask. He's also being haunted by that Blackwing spook!"

17 *Slaver's Fate*

The Hardy boys regarded Jack Wayne's customer with interest. "Would you mind telling us the whole story, Mr. Trask?" Frank requested. "As Jack says, my brother and I are trying to solve the mystery of that so-called flying ghost. If you've seen it, too, maybe you can give us some useful information."

"Be glad to help if I can," Trask replied. "I'd like to know the answer as much as you two. I don't like being made a fool of. What really worries me, though, is that that black contraption—whatever it is—may be part of a criminal scheme."

"What makes you think that, sir?" Joe asked.

The stocky businessman shrugged and frowned uneasily. "I've just formed a small electronics company. We're opening a plant near Hill Creek, and right now I'm in the process of negotiating an important defense contract with the Pentagon. The work we'll be doing is highly classified and involves very expensive materials—in other words, just the sort of thing that could attract thieves or industrial spies, maybe even foreign agents."

Frank said, "Does that mean you've seen the Blackwing ghost flying over your plant site?"

"Well, if that's what you call the thing. All I know is, it skims around at night on big black wings."

"How often has it appeared?"

"Twice. The first time was about a week ago. My plant's not in operation yet, you understand, and I went there one evening to inspect the layout and see how things were coming along. Just as I was leaving the building, I spotted this thing hovering overhead. I couldn't believe my eyes!" Trask shook his head incredulously as he reminisced. "It was a dark, cloudy night, and the thing flew off so silently, I almost decided it was just a trick of my imagination. But then I spotted it again the night before last, and this time I *knew* something was really up there."

Trask explained that he had come to the Ace Air Service office to get information on air charter rates for overnight shipments to Washington. When he happened to mention the weird incidents to Jack Wayne, the pilot immediately suggested that he get in touch with the Hardy boys.

"Have you told all this to the police?" Joe asked.

"Not yet." Tyler Trask looked embarrassed. "I was afraid they'd tell me to have my head examined."

"Well, *we* believe you, Mr. Trask—we've seen that flying black specter ourselves!"

"Look," said Frank, "if you spot it again, would you call us right away?" He wrote down his telephone number and handed it to the thick-set electronics manufacturer.

"You bet I will! I'm glad I met you fellows. This takes quite a load off my mind, just finding out for sure that I'm not suffering from hallucinations."

After chatting a few minutes longer, Trask left the office. The Hardy boys then asked Jack Wayne to try to find out more about the fighter pilot Max Kirby through his Air Force contacts.

"Sure thing," Jack promised. "Does this mean he may have had something to do with the Blackwing ghost?"

Frank grinned wryly. "Had or has—that past tense is the big question. First we have to find out for sure if he's dead or still alive."

When the Hardys drove home from the airport, they excitedly discussed the latest development in the Blackwing mystery.

"From what Trask told us," said Joe, "do you suppose his electronics plant could be the next target of the gang Dad's after?"

"Just what I'm wondering," Frank replied. "Let's try and raise Dad on the radio again. This could be important!"

Within two minutes after reaching the Hardys' house on Elm Street, the boys were beaming out an emergency-code call to their father.

This time Fenton Hardy responded promptly. He explained that following his earlier radio conversation with his sons, he had left the beach shack to replenish his supplies and to call a local FBI agent.

The famed sleuth listened closely as the boys related what they had learned from Tyler Trask. Though he was interested, he seemed doubtful that Trask's company was likely to be worth a break-in by the high-tech gang. "If the plant's not even in operation yet, I don't see what the thieves would stand to gain by robbing it. Even so, I'd say the lead should be followed up. Keep me informed, will you, of anything else you find out from Trask."

"Sure, Dad," Frank responded. Then he described the odd coincidences that had aroused the boys' interest in finding out more about Max Kirby and the disgruntled inventor who had lost his lawsuit against Technicom.

"Are you implying they may be one and the same person?" Mr. Hardy asked.

"We're not that suspicious—yet," Frank answered. "But they have cropped up in your case and in the Blackwing mystery, and it does seem strange the way certain evidence matches. You have always told us, Dad, that so-called coincidences bear looking into."

"True enough, son. I'll call the FBI in Washington right away. They should be able to give me a readout on that inventor." The sleuth advised Frank and Joe to come to the beach shack at about two o'clock that afternoon to see what he had learned—but to use every possible precaution to ensure that they weren't followed.

"Okay, Dad. We'll see you then." Frank signed off.

It was nearing noon when the Hardy boys returned to the house from their crime lab over the garage, and they were glad to notice that their mother and Aunt Gertrude were preparing lunch.

They flopped down in comfortable chairs in the living room while waiting to eat. Frank picked up the copy of *American Geographic* magazine that he had borrowed from the library and began reading the article about the old-time slave-ship captains. Almost at once the colorful details seized his interest.

"Boy, you should read this, Joe," he murmured, looking up from the magazine a short time later. "It even mentions Moray Thaw, the skipper who bought Blackwing Mansion."

"No kidding! What does it say about him?"

"He sounds like a real black-hearted villain. The guy not only made a business out of human misery, but after selling off his last cargo of slaves in Havana, he double-crossed his own mates and crew."

"How'd he do that?" asked Joe, getting up from his chair to peer over Frank's shoulder at the pictures in the magazine.

"Well, once a voyage was over and the cargo disposed of," Frank explained, "a slave-trading captain would normally split the profits with his

156

underlings according to the percentages they'd agreed on when they signed the ship's articles. Instead, this old buzzard flew the coop."

"You mean he sneaked out of Havana without paying them off?"

"Right. He made a getaway after dark on a fast racing sloop and was never seen again."

Joe chuckled dryly. "Sounds like some operator!"

"He was a close man with a buck, all right. The article says he'd made at least half a dozen successful slave-trading voyages before that last one, and each time he was known to have converted his profits into precious stones."

"Wow! The old crook must've had quite a bit of loot stashed away!"

Frank nodded. "Definitely. And not only that—the crew found out belatedly that he'd sold the ship itself, after removing its black-winged figurehead, while they were carousing ashore. So the money he received for the ship made another nice round sum to add to his retirement fund before he disappeared."

"Disappeared?" Joe echoed quizzically. "But Captain Blackwing didn't just vanish from the face of the earth after he sailed away from Havana. He came here to Bayport."

157

"Sure, we know that, but his crew didn't . . . and apparently neither did the writer of this article."

"Wash your hands and come to the table, you two!" Aunt Gertrude called out crisply from the dining room. "Don't let me have to tell you again, or your soup will get cold!"

The conversation at lunch concerned a new resort motel that was being built overlooking Barmet Bay, and an elaborate patchwork quilt Mrs. Hardy and Aunt Gertrude were working on together. It wasn't until Frank and Joe were on their way to the beach shack to meet their father that the boys got around again to the subject of the old slaving skipper.

"You know something, Frank?" Joe mused aloud as they drove along the Shore Road. "If Captain Thaw did retire with a huge fortune, the old buzzard could have hidden it somewhere in Blackwing Mansion."

Frank nodded thoughtfully. "It's possible, and that *might* have something to do with the Blackwing ghost. On the other hand, don't forget what that newspaper feature on the mansion said, about the old man being found dead with a look of terror on his face."

"Meaning what?"

"It might mean one or more of his old ship-mates tracked him down, bent on revenge—and Thaw died of a heart attack brought on by sheer fright."

Joe whistled. "And if they made him talk before he kicked the bucket, they could have walked off with the treasure!"

"Exactly . . . which would also explain why the loot didn't turn up when the Allens had the mansion restored."

The brothers parked off the Shore Road, as Biff Hooper had done with his van during their previous visit, and then walked across the dunes to the shack.

Somewhat to their surprise, the door was standing ajar.

"Dad?" Joe called out.

Receiving no answer, the boys hurried inside—only to stop short in sudden shock.

The cabin's interior was in wild disarray. The table and chairs were knocked over, and Marlin-spike McGee's few belongings were scattered about the bare plank floor! Fenton Hardy was nowhere in sight!

18 Stakeout

Wide-eyed with alarm, the brothers scanned anxiously for clues to the struggle that had evidently taken place.

"Look!" Joe cried, dropping to one knee and pointing to several dark reddish stains on the floor. "Blood spots!"

"Good grief!" Frank examined them closely and touched one with his finger. "Still sticky—so it can't have happened very long ago!"

Joe looked at his older brother for guidance. "What should we do, Frank—call the police?"

"Don't worry, my boys. That won't be necessary."

The young detectives whirled, relief replacing surprise as they recognized the deep, reassuring voice behind them.

"Dad!" Joe exclaimed, leaping up to grip his father's hand as Mr. Hardy walked in through the doorway. "Are you okay?"

"There's blood on your shirt!" Frank added worriedly.

"Just a scratch." The famed manhunter explained that after going out to call FBI headquarters from a shorefront phone, he had returned to find Ranse Hobb ransacking the cabin.

"What happened?" asked Joe.

"Quite a brawl, as you can see from the looks of this place. Hobb finally jabbed me with a knife and got away. I went after him, but—" Fenton Hardy grinned apologetically—"I guess the shock and pain of the wound were too much for me. I keeled over on the sand and just came to a few minutes ago. By then, of course, Hobb was nowhere in sight."

"Sit down, Dad," Frank insisted, "and let's get a look at that cut." He opened his father's shirt to expose the knife wound. Although it was severe enough to be very painful, apparently no vital organs had been damaged.

While Joe ran to get the first-aid kit from their

car, Frank boiled some water he got from the rusty pump outside. In fifteen minutes the cut had been swabbed with antiseptic and bandaged.

"What did you find out from the FBI, Dad?" Joe inquired as they set about restoring order to the cabin. "Any word yet on that inventor?"

"Yes, indeed. They had already checked him out, so it was just a matter of pulling information from the case file. By the way, are you two ready for another shock?"

Frank grinned. "Try us."

"The inventor's name was—Max Kirby."

Both boys gasped with excitement. "So Frank's hunch was right!" Joe cried out.

"What about the lawsuit?" his older brother asked. "Any details on that?"

"It concerned the patent rights to a new type of engine silencer Kirby had invented." Mr. Hardy's words brought another excited response from his sons.

"A silencer would help explain the Blackwing mystery!" Joe declared.

Fenton Hardy nodded. "You two have scored another bull's-eye."

"How come Kirby had to start a lawsuit over his invention?" Frank pursued.

162

"It seems Technicom imposed certain legal technicalities over the patent to keep his invention off the market."

"Why?" asked Joe.

"Because the corporation already owns a highly profitable automotive muffler company, and they didn't want their investment in that business wiped out overnight by Kirby's revolutionary new silencer."

Joe shook his head reflectively. "No wonder he got so sore at Technicom!"

Frank asked, "Did the FBI conclude that he died in an accident?"

"Well, apparently the local authorities did," Mr. Hardy replied. "Going by the evidence, his car crashed through a bridge rail at night into a fast-flowing river. His body was never recovered, yet the police report made it more or less official that he'd drowned."

Joe socked his fist into his open palm. "But he could have faked his own death and then developed a black ultralight, with an engine muffled by his own highly advanced silencer."

"Which he then used to carry out a series of high-tech robberies," Frank concluded, "including raids on three separate plants owned by Technicom, Inc."

Fenton Hardy frowned and nodded as he rubbed his jaw thoughtfully. "It makes a convincing theory, all right."

"Dad, if your hunch is right that Ross Robotics will be the next robbery target, why wait for the Black Butterfly to attack it?" Frank argued.

"You're suggesting we bait a trap for him?"

"Right!" Frank outlined a scheme that had just occurred to him.

Both his father and Joe added suggestions of their own, and eventually Mr. Hardy agreed that the idea was worth a try. If plant officials and law-enforcement authorities agreed, he would urge them to put the plan into action that very night.

Meanwhile, partly to kill time, Frank and Joe drove to the office of the Bayport *News* to interview the reporter who had written the feature articles on the Blackwing Mansion, Jerry Lynch.

Lynch was interested to learn what the *American Geographic* piece said about Captain Blackwing. "I wish I'd read that before I wrote my features on the mansion," he remarked. "It would have made them twice as interesting!"

"Do you think Thaw's old shipmates may have hunted him down?" Joe asked.

"Sure! That's the likeliest explanation for that

look of terror on his face. The original news story about his death that I dug up indicated that he may have had visitors just before he died. A bottle of rum was uncorked and had been knocked over. There were no drinking glasses in sight, but if his visitors were old sea dogs like himself, they might not have bothered drinking from glasses."

Before the Hardy boys left, Lynch pulled out an interesting object from his desk drawer.

"What's that?" Frank inquired.

"An old-fashioned belaying pin. These things fit into holes in the fife rail around a sailing ship's main mast, and various rigging lines were attached or belayed to them. They also made a convenient weapon in case a deckhand got sassy to an officer or the bosun."

The belaying pin Lynch was showing the boys consisted of a cylindrical iron bar with an ivory grip fitted over it, like a tool handle. "The Allens gave it to me as a souvenir," Lynch added, "after I finished writing the feature stories on the mansion."

Frank hefted the heavy gadget. "You mean this *belonged* to Captain Blackwing?"

"Apparently so. They ran across it when the mansion was being restored. As a matter of fact, that old news story mentioned that a belaying pin was lying close at hand when the captain's body was found sprawled on the floor—so he was probably using it to defend himself."

Joe pointed to the decorative carving on the ivory handle. "It's been scrimshawed."

"Right. Since you know the word, I guess you know that's an art that was practiced by seamen on whaling cruises."

Frank glanced at the reporter. "Say, would you mind lending us this for a while if we take good care of it?"

Lynch grinned and flapped his hand carelessly. "Be my guest."

That afternoon the management of Ross Robotics made a public announcement that was carried on the evening news. The company president told a group of reporters that his organization had just developed a new type of microprocessor that would accelerate the automation of industrial plants.

"I have here," he said, showing them a plastic box studded with several knobs and dials, "a master control unit embodying the new microprocessor. With this device a single engineer will be able to monitor and control an entire factory production line. This pilot model will be flown to Washington tomorrow morning for demonstration to a number of officials from the U.S. Commerce and Defense departments."

The Hardy boys grinned after listening to the televised press conference.

"The trap's baited," Frank said.

Shortly after dark the two young sleuths left the house and drove out to Highway 19 in their yellow sports sedan. After turning off the highway just before the Ross Robotics plant, they parked on a deserted side street and made their way on foot toward the factory grounds.

For the next half hour they prowled about in the darkness, carefully scouting all approaches to the plant as well as various vantage points from which to keep watch on whatever happened. At last they chose a patch of shrubbery across the road and a few hundred yards from the main gate. Here they settled down to hide and await developments.

"No sign of the police yet, or the FBI," Joe remarked after a while.

"No, and my hunch is there won't be any," Frank said. "They probably staked out the plant from the inside before the press conference was even held."

An hour went by; then another. Time seemed

to drag more and more slowly as the boys crouched and waited for the trap to be sprung. Soon after ten P.M. and again at eleven-fifteen, the Hardys had to stand to their full height and stretch their aching limbs, hoping they would not be seen.

"Think the gang sensed that the whole thing is a setup?" Joe wondered gloomily.

"We won't know till the night's over," Frank replied with a rueful grin.

As midnight neared, the boys stiffened to attention at the rumbling sound of an approaching tractor-trailer.

"Where's it coming from?" Frank muttered, straining his eyes in the dark.

"Carter Road, I think," Joe said, referring to the route that led to the plant entrance. "But something tells me the driver's operating without lights. This must be it, Frank!"

Both boys tensed when they heard the heavy vehicle slow for a moment, then start up again with a roar, as if the driver had just gunned the engine to full power.

An instant later the plant's own floodlights revealed a huge truck speeding out of the darkness toward the main gates!

With an earsplitting crash, the juggernaut

rammed into the closed steel gates and exploded in a ball of fire!

The blast sent shock waves echoing in all directions, like an earthshaking clap of thunder! The truck was a tanker, and its load of fuel had evidently ignited on impact. Flames shot high in the air, and dense fumes were soon billowing outward from the scene of the crash.

For a moment the Hardys were too stunned to speak. Then, as they stared at the ominously flaring spectacle, Joe gasped, "No driver!"

"The truck slowed down for a second or two, remember?" said Frank. "The driver probably opened the door of the cab and got ready to hop out just before he gunned the engine—maybe with a hand throttle."

"That figures, all right. He must've been carrying an explosive or a detonator to set off that big a blast!"

The dingy factory area around the plant was largely deserted at this late hour. Even so, a few lights had come on in nearby buildings in response to the ear-shattering explosion, and people were soon running outdoors to find out what had happened. The Hardy boys emerged from their hiding place and approached the plant gates, but the waves of heat radiating outward from the blazing tanker rig prevented them from going too close.

By now security guards and others—presumably police or FBI stakeouts—were running toward the fiery scene at the entrance to Ross Robotics. The main building, however, remained in darkness, and Joe suddenly realized that even the fence and ground lights, which had not been damaged by the blast, had gone dark.

"The main power line's been cut!" he exclaimed, snapping his fingers.

"You're right!" Frank said. "That means all the plant's burglar alarms and other security devices are no longer working!"

The scream of fire sirens ripped through the night air. Within moments fire trucks from Bayport and adjoining communities were converging on the inferno. Hoses were unreeled, and powerful streams of water were soon playing over the blaze. The spread of the flames was quickly halted, but the tanker wreckage was already glowing white-hot, and the combustion temperature was obviously too high for the fire to be extinguished.

"We'll have to let it burn itself out!" the Bayport fire chief shouted to one of the policemen who was helping to keep the onlookers at a safe distance from the blaze.

"I wish we could find Dad!" Joe muttered, looking around in helpless frustration.

"So do I," Frank said.

With the plant gateway effectively blocked by the fire, there was no way to get inside the grounds short of climbing the high security fence that surrounded the building. With the electricity off, the brothers decided to risk it.

Frank was first to scale the barrier. However, when he was about to pull himself over the fence, he found himself staring into the gun of a security guard inside the compound.

"Stop!" the man shouted.

19 Mansion Raid

Rather than explain to the security guard that he was not a lawbreaking intruder, Frank quickly retreated.

"We might as well wait here until Dad comes out," he told his brother when the two boys were on the ground again. "It—"

He stopped short when suddenly lights came on along the fence and grounds and in several windows of the main building. Obviously power had been restored.

"Hey, there's Chief Collig!" Joe cried a moment later. "Maybe he can fill us in."

He waved to the police chief, who was a long-time friend of the Hardy family. "Is Dad still inside?" Joe asked.

"Yes, up in the research lab," the chief replied. "The place was burgled while the power, was off, and the master control unit's gone!" He was scowling and red-faced with anger at the way the baited trap had been circumvented by the thieves' fiery trickery.

As he strode off toward the gate, Joe looked at his brother with a wry grin. "Boy, whoever pulled this job had better not fall into Collig's clutches!"

"You said it! The chief looked mad enough to make hamburger out of him." Even though the control device was actually in the crude early stages of development and had been shown on TV only as bait to snare the high-tech plant robbery gang, it still contained valuable trade-secret microchips. Its theft, therefore, was a damaging blow to Chief Collig's professional pride.

Frank's expression became serious and thoughtful. "Do you suppose our theory was all wrong about the Black Butterfly being the crook who pulls these high-tech plant raids?"

173

he mused aloud.

Joe shook his head emphatically. "No way. The guy's smart, that's all. He knew Dad was in the Bayport area, so he took no chances on the Ross Robotics publicity being a trap. He may or may not have used his flying rig tonight. The point is, the power blackout made it easy to get in and out of the plant and raid the research lab without triggering any alarm, while everyone's attention was distracted by the explosion and fire at the gate."

Frank nodded. "Okay, that's the way I see it, too, so let's take it a step further. If we're right, will the Black Butterfly and the gang he's working with want to hang around Bayport much longer?"

"Not if they use their heads. They must know the cops will have an all-points bulletin on the police wire right now, and by morning the FBI and the state police will have a dragnet out over this whole area. The smart thing would be to get out of town pronto."

"Exactly! But if the rest of our theory's right, the Black Butterfly's got his eye on another score here in Bayport."

Joe snapped his fingers and stared at his brother excitedly. "You're right, Frank! And right now would be a perfect time to go after it, while the police are concentrating all their efforts on the Ross Robotics job!"

"So what are we standing around here for? Come on—let's go!"

The Hardys raced back to their sports sedan and took off with a *vrooom!* of exhaust. Minutes later they were whizzing along Indian Road. At Joe's suggestion, Frank braked to a stop well short of their destination, to avoid announcing their arrival. The boys then leaped out of the car and sprinted the rest of the way to the Blackwing Mansion.

The sinister gatepost figure loomed overhead as they turned up the driveway. Both brothers stopped short with audible gasps at the sight that greeted their eyes beyond the entrance shrubbery.

On the smooth expanse of lawn to the right of the old house stood a black ultralight aircraft!

"The ghost must be inside!" Joe hissed.

"Right—so don't make a sound!"

Lights glowed behind the closed drapes of the living room windows. As they mounted the steps to the veranda, the Hardys noticed at once that the door was not fully closed. It opened at Frank's gentle push to reveal another startling sight.

Jeff Allen lay on the floor of the vestibule, gagged and bound! Without a word the two boys rushed to untie him.

"See about Mary!" Allen urged in a low, anxious whisper as soon as the gag was removed.

His wife was tied on the sofa in the living room. When they were freed, the couple poured out their story. After returning late from a dinner party at a friend's house, they had switched on the television and were watching a news bulletin on the fiery tanker crash at Ross Robotics when they heard the doorbell ring.

Jeff Allen went to answer it. Seeing no one outside, he stepped onto the veranda to look around and was promptly felled by a blow on the head. He was then dragged inside and bound.

Any noise from the assault was drowned out by the television news audio, so Mary Allen was unaware of what had happened to her husband. With her back turned as she watched the TV screen, she, too, was easy prey for the intruder. Neither had even glimpsed their assailant. "But he may still be in the house!" Jeff warned.

"He's here, all right," Joe said. "His black

176

wings are parked right outside."

"But what on earth is he up to?" asked Mrs. Allen in a frightened whisper.

"If our hunch is right," Frank explained softly, "he's looking for a treasure that was hidden here years ago by Captain Moray Thaw."

The Hardys quickly related what they had learned about the old slaver, including the way he had double-crossed his own crew and fled from Cuba to the United States with a fortune in jewels and cash.

Jeff Allen frowned and shook his head doubtfully. "If that's what the creep's after, he's out of luck. Any treasure that was stashed in the house would surely have turned up when we had this place restored. Every single room was redone—even the attic was wired and insulated!"

"What about the basement?" asked Joe. "Remember, this used to be a station on the Underground Railway before the Civil War. That means there was probably a place for hiding the runaway slaves."

Mr. and Mrs. Allen looked at each other somewhat less certainly and ended by shrugging. "The basement was waterproofed and then finished off with wood paneling and tiles,"

Jeff said. "If there was any secret underground room, I don't see how we could have missed it, right, Mary?"

Mrs. Allen agreed.

"Well, never mind—we'll worry about that later," Frank said. "The important thing is that that creep who attacked you tonight is probably the phony ghost who's been bugging you all along. And if our hunch is right, it's Blackwing's treasure that he's after. Seems to me the basement is one of the places he's apt to look first."

"Could be the guy's armed," Joe pointed out. "Maybe we'd better not go hunting for him empty-handed!"

"Wait!" Mrs. Allen said worriedly. "Shouldn't we call the police?"

Frank nodded. "Good thinking."

She hurried to the phone and started to dial, then flashed a glance of dismay at the others. "The line's dead!"

Without a word Frank took out the ivory-handled belaying pin he had borrowed from the *News* reporter. Joe picked up a poker from the fireplace, and Jeff Allen armed himself with a golf club. "The crook may have heard us moving around," Frank cautioned, "so let's tiptoe from here on."

The trio made their way silently to the kitchen, with Mrs. Allen following close behind. The door to the basement landing was open and the stairway light was on, indicating that the Hardys had correctly guessed the raider's move.

Frank signaled the others to pause and listen. Sure enough, faint sounds could be heard coming from below. After a whispered conference, it was decided not to risk a head-on assault but instead to let the intruder show himself and then try to take him by surprise.

The group had not long to wait. Soon steps were heard mounting the stairs. Allen poised himself on one side of the basement doorway, the Hardys on the other.

A black-clad figure came into view, clutching a flashlight in one hand and a black bag that looked like a toolkit in the other. Before he realized what was happening, the three lurking avengers hurled him to the floor and pinioned his arms and legs.

The prisoner was wearing a zippered black jumpsuit and a black hood with eye holes. Joe pulled off the hood, then gasped.

"It's the butterfly collector who came to see Mr. Drexel!"

"Saxby," Frank said. "But something tells me

179

his real name is Max Kirby!"

The dark-haired, hazel-eyed crook was allowed to sit upright after his wrists and ankles were securely tied. But his only response to the Hardys' grilling was a mocking grin. "Sorry, guys, but you'll get no help from me."

"Okay," Frank said, losing patience. "You can do your talking to the police and the FBI. Our dad, Fenton Hardy, can supply all the details about your past that they'll need to identify you and send you to jail, including your fake drowning and your legal hassles with Technicom, Inc."

For the first time Kirby-alias-Saxby's arrogant manner seemed to falter.

"And there are Air Force vets who can identify you as the Black Butterfly," Joe added.

The Hardys suspected that the prisoner's search for Captain Blackwing's treasure had not been successful. As Frank reached out to pick up the belaying pin, which he had laid down on the floor temporarily, his brother suddenly stopped him. "Hold it a second, Frank!"

"What's the matter?"

"Let me see the scrimshawing on that ivory handle."

With a puzzled expression, the older Hardy

boy handed over the belaying pin. Joe examined it, then looked up excitedly. "Did you notice that carving on the oak wall panels when we came through the dining room?"

"Not particularly."

Joe sprang to his feet and strode out of the kitchen, followed by Frank and the Allens. "The carving on these wall panels," he pointed out when they reached the dining room, "shows a shield with stars and stripes on it, surmounted by the head of an eagle, with fancy scrollwork underneath, like a coat of arms."

Jeff Allen nodded. "So?"

"Now look at the scrimshawing on the ivory handle of this belaying pin. It's the same design!"

"You're right!"

"And the eye of the eagle in both cases has sparks shooting out from it, so that it seems almost like a star," Frank added. "That has to be more than just a coincidence!"

Allen looked at the Hardys expectantly. "But what does it mean?"

"If it *is* more than a coincidence," Joe reasoned, "it must mean either that Captain Thaw did the scrimshawing himself to resemble the wall carving, or else he had a carver copy the scrimshaw design on the wall panels."

Frank rubbed his jaw, frowning thoughtfully. "Okay, that figures, but it still doesn't tell us *why*." He glanced up at Mr. and Mrs. Allen. "How much do you know about this belaying pin?"

Jeff Allen shrugged. "Nothing. We just found it lying around after we bought the house."

Mary Allen said, "Well, one of the neighbors did say something about it—old Mrs. Hemming, who lives across the street. She dropped over for a visit one day, and I showed her the belaying pin. When she saw it she told me a story she'd heard from her grandfather years and years ago. It seems Captain Blackwing was up on the widow's walk one day and suffered a slight stroke—in fact, he almost fell off and was seen hanging over the railing, unconscious. A doctor was called, and the captain had to be nursed back to health, but during that time he lost part of his memory due to the stroke and couldn't even recall his own name."

"Bet the old curmudgeon hated that!" Jeff commented.

"Apparently so. The story goes that after he finally recovered, he was more cantankerous than ever. Whenever he appeared outside the house, he was always clutching that belaying pin, as if he was ready to use it on anyone who came snooping around his property."

Joe slammed his fist into his open palm and shot an excited glance at his brother. "That would fit right in, don't you see? Maybe after he suffered his stroke, he couldn't remember where he'd hidden his treasure. So he scrimshawed this design on the ivory handle as a reminder, in case the same thing ever happened again!"

"You've hit it, Joe!" Frank looked equally excited. "And I think I've just clued in on the rest of it!"

"What do you mean?"

"Look here at the end of the handle. See these little dots carved into the ivory? Do you recognize the constellation they form?"

"The Big Dipper!" Joe blurted.

"Right! And the two outer stars in the pan are pointing toward the eagle's eye—"

"Which would make that the North Star!"

Frank nodded. "What's more, this room is octagonal in shape, and—let's see, now—over there would be the north panel!"

The boys strode toward it, followed by Mr. and Mrs. Allen. Frank ran his hands over the panel, then, on a sudden impulse, pressed the eagle's eye. The next moment Mary Allen uttered a startled cry.

The wall panel was swinging outward!

20 *Blackwing's Secret*

The open wall panel revealed a flight of stone steps leading downward into darkness.

"Wait'll I get Kirby's flashlight!" said Joe.

He returned in a moment, and the group started down the steps with the yellow brilliance of the flashlight beam illuminating their way.

"Judging by the length of this stairway, it must lead below the basement," Jeff Allen muttered in surprise.

The steps ended in a stone-walled chamber. Joe played the flashlight about the room, revealing half a dozen boxlike cots filled with moldy straw, plus a bare plank table and benches to sit on.

"The hideout for the runaway slaves!" Mary Allen exclaimed in an awed voice.

On the table lay a small brass chest. The Hardys rushed toward it, and Frank flipped up the lid. The chest was stuffed with old-fashioned U.S. greenbacks and a handful of glittering jewels—diamonds, sapphires, emeralds and rubies!

All four gaped at the trove with sharp intakes of breath. Frank found his voice first. "Well, well, well! Thaw's crew may have tracked him down and scared him to death, but one thing's sure—they never got their hooks on his treasure!"

"Nice work, my boys!" A chuckling voice suddenly sounded above them. "You've just saved us the trouble of finding it."

The Hardys and Allens whirled. The speaker was a stocky, broad-shouldered man with iron-gray hair, his face creased in a mocking smile. He was standing at the top of the stone steps, just inside the wall panel opening. With him was a tough-looking dark-bearded thug whose close-cropped reddish hair grew low on his forehead.

186

"Tyler Trask and Ranse Hobb!" Frank exclaimed in a low, tense voice.

Trask's wolfish smile widened. "No need for introductions, I see. Good! That simplifies matters. If you know anything about Hobb's criminal record, then you know he's the kind of enforcer who'll stop at nothing. And that device he's holding, as you probably know, is a flame thrower—which he's ready to use, I might add, on those straw cots down there if any of you make a move!"

There was a moment of grim silence as his menacing words sank in. Then Trask chuckled again. "Now then, if you all understand those basic facts, let's be brisk and businesslike. I believe the young lady there may be the best one to pick up the treasure chest and bring it to me—while the rest of you stay perfectly still, with your hands in the air! Understand?" -

"Wait a minute!" Joe broke in. "How do you figure in this high-tech robbery racket, Trask? I thought you told us at the Ace Air Service office that you were about to open an electronics plant of your own."

"Just a line to string you along. I knew your old man often employed Jack Wayne as a pilot, so I planned to set a trap for you Hardys—but now you've saved me the trouble. Apparently an introduction *is* needed, after all."

"Don't bother," Joe rasped. "If the name Tyler Trask was just an alias, that means you must be—"

"Klaus Kane!" said Frank. "The international ‚crook and arms dealer the FBI and CIA are both after!"

The heavyset criminal inclined his head slightly in a mocking bow. "My reputation, it seems, has preceded me. Well, that, too, should save time, since you know I'm prepared to kill any awkward fools who get in my way."

"What about Max Kirby?" said Frank. "Do you intend to kill him, too—or is he still working for you?"

"He *was* working for me, but the treacherous fool got a little too clever for his own good—or rather *thought* he was being clever. So I'm afraid we may have to dispose of the Black Butterfly permanently before we leave Blackwing Mansion. Meanwhile, young lady"—Kane's piercing gaze swung from the Hardys toward Mary Allen—"I suggest you do as I say and hand up that brass chest to me!"

As if to emphasize his boss's command, Ranse Hobb aimed his flamethrower at the little group clustered in the underground chamber.

But the next moment Hobb himself was tumbling down the stone steps! Max Kirby, though he was still bound hand and foot, had hopped to the wall-panel opening and butted the thug with his head!

Jeff Allen, who was closest to the foot of the stairway, reacted fast. He dived for the flame-thrower, which had slipped from Hobb's grasp as he fell. But the thug also recovered and came back quickly. He swung a wild haymaker at Allen's jaw and knocked him off his feet.

Klaus Kane, meanwhile, smashed a furious punch at the Black Butterfly, which sent him toppling over backward into the dining room. Joe Hardy brushed Mrs. Allen aside and leaped up the stone steps to attack the master criminal with both fists flying. At the same time Frank launched himself like a wildcat at Ranse Hobb.

Kane kicked out at Joe, who grabbed him by the foot, and both went rolling and buffeting downstairs. Jeff Allen had been stunned momentarily by Hobb's roundhouse uppercut, but Frank, after trading punches with the thug, reached across Allen, trying to snatch up the flamethrower and use it as a weapon. Hobb lashed out with another blow to thwart the move.

Mary Allen was forced to back away from the

wild fracas to keep from being hurt by the blows and kicks that were being exchanged. The outcome of the struggle was still in doubt when the deep, authoritative voice of Fenton Hardy barked a command from the top of the stairway.

"Kane! Hobb! On your feet, you two, and stand with your hands pressed against the wall—up high where we can see them!"

The private investigator was accompanied by two law officers. One kept the crooks covered while the other frisked them and then applied handcuffs.

"How'd you get here, Dad?" Frank asked in relief.

"Chief Collig told me he'd seen you two at the Ross Robotics plant, and I figured this was where you'd head next." Mr. Hardy grinned at his sons. "I guess our minds work the same way."

The boys told him how Max Kirby had toppled Hobb in the nick of time.

Fenton Hardy nodded. "That'll certainly count in his favor when he comes to trial."

Seeing that the game was up, the crooked pilot shrugged and talked freely, even offering to turn state's evidence against the others in hope of receiving a lighter sentence.

Kirby stated that he had turned criminal out of sheer anger and frustration after losing his lawsuit against Technicom. He confessed that he had been working in cahoots with Kane and Hobb for over a year. He had carried out the high-tech plant raids by means of his black ultralight, which he was able to fly without engine noise because of the silencer he had invented.

Klaus Kane bought the stolen technical data and hardware from him and sold it to unscrupulous foreign buyers. He in turn paid Kirby partly in money and partly in valuable butterfly specimens that were stolen by Ranse Hobb from various collections around the country.

"You're a butterfly fancier yourself?" Joe queried.

The pilot nodded and grinned sardonically. "Yes, a rabid one. In fact, you might say I've been hooked on butterflies ever since I was a kid. I'm well known to other collectors, you see, and sometimes I'd even go and see their collections and pick out the exact specimens I wanted stolen. But when Hobb pulled off the actual burglary, I'd be far away in another state, with an ironclad alibi, so I never even came under suspicion."

"And the silver butterfly ornament that was caught in the tree branch outside Blackwing Mansion was yours, I presume?" Joe queried.

"Yes, I started wearing that as a good-luck charm while I was flying as a mercenary in Africa."

"How come you picked a *Prepona deiphile* as a model for the ornament?" Frank asked curiously.

"My dad was a pilot, too," Kirby replied. "He brought me back a real *Prepona* after a flight to Brazil, when I first got interested in butterflies. *Prepona*s are fast fliers, you know, so it became my favorite specimen."

While reading the article about *Prepona* butterflies in *American Geographic* magazine, Kirby had run across the feature on slave-ship captains just as Frank did. "I was in Bayport about a year ago," the pilot went on. "Just about the time those newspaper stories on the Blackwing Mansion were published. I immediately realized that Captain Thaw's treasure might still be hidden somewhere in the house."

"Of course!" Mary Allen broke in. "Now I recognize you! You're the stranger who offered to buy the house from us."

Kirby nodded again. "That's right. And when

you wouldn't sell, I decided to try scaring you out of the house." He explained that the ghostly voice of the dead slave-ship captain had come from radio speakers hidden inside the walls of certain rooms, adding, "I managed to plant them there at night while the house was undergoing restoration."

After a number of visits to Bayport while carrying out the machinations of his plot, Kirby finally decided to quit the high-tech robbery racket. Klaus Kane, however, pursued him to Bayport, fearful that he might be planning to contact Fenton Hardy secretly and double-cross his former partners by testifying against them in exchange for a promise of immunity from prosecution.

After a heated argument and various threats by Kane, Kirby had agreed to help terrorize the Hardys and pull one last job, which turned out to be the raid on the Ross Robotics plant.

But secretly Max Kirby had had a game plan of his own. While Ranse Hobb caused the tank truck to crash into the entrance gate and then cut the main power line, Kirby landed his black ultralight in the darkest corner of the plant grounds and swiftly snatched the master control device from the research lab. When he brought the loot, however, to the agreed-on pickup spot, he delivered it in a booby-trapped flight bag. He was hoping that the delayed-action bomb concealed inside would get the other two crooks off his back forever.

Klaus Kane, though, was too cagey and suspicious to fall victim to such a plot. He had discovered and deactivated the bomb and then followed the Black Butterfly to the Allen mansion.

The next morning Chet Morton and other friends of Frank and Joe came to the Hardys' house to hear about the night's exciting events. The news headlines and telecasts had whetted their appetite for firsthand details.

Just as Frank and Joe were finishing their story, Sam Radley arrived. After congratulating the boys, he added, "I thought you might want to know about Matt Creech. That joker you spotted him with at the waterfront café turned out to be one of the biggest drug smugglers on the East Coast. Creech was flying in some of the shipments, and he thought you two were on to him."

"Wow!" said Joe. "No wonder he had it in for us! Where is he now, Sam?"

"They're both behind bars. And incidentally, Jonas Milgrim and Clyde Peachum may wind up in jail, too—thanks to that investigator, Nagel. They're now being grilled by the DA on charges of using fraud and coercion in negotiating various real estate deals. Milgrim's already admitted that Peachum hired him to bulldoze the Allens into selling their house."

Joe grinned at his brother. "Looks like we can wrap up the Blackwing mystery, eh, Frank?"

"Hey, that's not all!" Chet broke in. "Mr. Drexel retrieved his stolen butterfly from those crooks, and he says you guys will get the five-thousand-dollar reward he promised. How are you going to spend it?"

"Hmm . . . good question," Frank mused. "Perhaps we'll buy materials to build a new ultralight." He had no idea that this project would have to be postponed, however, since soon the boys would need all their spare time to investigate *The Swamp Monster*.

NANCY DREW® MYSTERY STORIES By Carolyn Keene

WATCH OUT FOR...
BILL WALLACE

Award winning author Bill Wallace brings you fun-filled stories of animals full of humor and exciting adventures.

☐ **BEAUTY** .... 68272/$2.95

☐ **RED DOG** .... 65750/$2.50

☐ **TRAPPED IN DEATH CAVE** .... 62851/$2.50

☐ **A DOG CALLED KITTY** .... 63969/$2.50

☐ **DANGER ON PANTHER PEAK** ... 61282/$2.50

☐ **SNOT STEW** .... 69335/$2.75

☐ **FERRET IN THE BEDROOM, LIZARDS IN THE FRIDGE** ...... 68099/$2.75

MINSTREL BOOKS™

JAMIE GILSON KEEPS YOU LAUGHING!

___ **HOBIE HANSON, YOU'RE WEIRD** 63971/$2.75
Who said being weird isn't any fun? Hobie Hanson
doesn't think so.

___ **DO BANANAS CHEW GUM?** 68259/$2.75
It's not a riddle, it's a test. And since Sam can't read, it's not
as easy as it looks!

___ **THIRTEEN WAYS TO SINK A SUB** 68427/$2.75
Substitute teachers are fair game–and the boys and girls of
Room 4B can't wait to play!

___ **4B GOES WILD** 68063/$2.75
The hilarious sequel to THIRTEEN WAYS TO SINK A SUB–Room
4B goes into the woods at Camp Trotter and has a wild time!

___ **HARVEY THE BEER CAN KING** 67423/$2.50
Harvey calls himself the Beer Can King, and why not? He's the
proud owner of 800 choice cans. A collection his dad would love
to throw in the trash!

___ **HELLO, MY NAME IS SCRAMBLED EGGS** 67039/$2.75
Making new friends should always be this much fun.

___ **CAN'T CATCH ME, I'M THE GINGERBREAD MAN**
69160/$2.75 Mitch was a hotshot hockey player, a health
food nut and a heavy favorite to win the National
bake-a-thon!

___ **DOUBLE DOG DARE** 67898/$2.75
Hobie has got to take a risk to prove he is special, too!

____**THE DASTARDLY MURDER OF DIRTY PETE**
   Eth Clifford 68859/$2.75
____**ME, MY GOAT, AND MY SISTER'S WEDDING**
   Stella Pevsner 66206/$2.75
____**DANGER ON PANTHER PEAK**
   Bill Marshall 70271/$2.95
____**BOWSER THE BEAUTIFUL**
   Judith Hollands 70488/$2.75
____**THE MONSTER'S RING**
   Bruce Colville 69389/$2.75
____**KEVIN CORBETT EATS FLIES**
   Patricia Hermes 69183/$2.95
____**ROSY COLE'S GREAT AMERICAN GUILT CLUB**
   Sheila Greenwald 70864/$2.75
____**ROSY'S ROMANCE** Sheila Greenwald 70292/$2.75
____**WRITE ON, ROSY!** Sheila Greenwald 68569/$2.75
____**ME AND THE TERRIBLE TWO** Ellen Conford 68491/$2.75
____**SNOT STEW** Bill Wallace 69335/$2.75
____**WHO NEEDS A BRATTY BROTHER?**
   Linda Gondosh 62777/$2.50
____**FERRET IN THE BEDROOM, LIZARDS IN THE FRIDGE**
   Bill Wallace 68009/$2.75
____**THE CASE OF THE VISITING VAMPIRE**
   Drew Stevenson 65732/$2.50
____**THE WITCHES OF HOPPER STREET**
   Linda Gondosch 64066/$2.50
____**HARVEY THE BEER CAN KING** Jamie Gilson 67423/$2.50
____**ALVIN WEBSTER'S SUREFIRE PLAN FOR SUCCESS**
   (AND HOW IT FAILED) Sheila Greenwald 67239/$2.75
____**THE KETCHUP SISTERS:**
   THE RESCUE OF THE RED-BLOODED LIBRARIAN
   Judith Hollands 66810/$2.75
____**THE KETCHUP SISTERS:**
   THE SECRET OF THE HAUNTED DOGHOUSE
   Judith Hollands 66812/$2.75